praise for alexander schaal:

>... fast, funny, going places ...<

>... the hottest writer in business

>... no end of wacky wonders ...<

> ... if you beginning to think - read this ...<

> A line manager is a nicely shaded creation, a moral man who is also all too human. Kill it is a slendid read, clever and provoking.<

with best wishes

It's a Monday morning and you're starting a new chapter in your life. There's something familiar about this book as soon as you delve into the first page.

You're aware that you're at the centre of something genuinely important, and the really exciting thing is to think that part of your job is going to be to try to establish where that centre is and also exactly what it's in the middle of.

Looks like a Beagle Boy

Buy it. Read it!

What does that involve exactly? Ask your line manager, ask yourself. Ask me. And underneath it all is probably one of the corporation's world most strategic directors. You! There's just a knack to it. Come and find the world of business, laugh, and have a funny workday.

The question we ask ourselves daily is, how would it be if things didn't have to be the way we know they actually are, right? What would a world look like if it was different?

And then it´s the weekend.

No path is too far for the business, no trend too new. Everything is freshly invented. Nothing ever works better. But the budget is exhausted. Only those who know themselves can lead others. But who has time for that, in the daily struggle to climb the career ladder?

The author Alexander Schaal is a biologist. His goal: to work with primates! Today he is a trainer, coach and interim manager. For the people and with the people. Mission accomplished! To joy and rediscovering new things!

Alexander Schaal

for Ashley and Karen - it wouldn´t have been finished without you

Kill it, from big fish and fat cats from alexander schaal.
Published in Germany in 2022, March by Amazon Books Copyright © Alexander Schaal and >11statt12 Verlag.< Alexander Schaal has asserted his right under the Copyright, Designs and Patents Act, 2022 to be identified as the author of this work This short story's are a work of fiction. Names and characters are the product of the author's imagination and any resemblance to actual persons, living or dead, is entirely coincidental is This book is sold subject to the condition that it shall not, by way of trade or otherwise, be lent, resold, hired out, or otherwise circulated without the publisher's prior consent in any form of binding or cover other than that in which it is published and without a similar condition including this condition being imposed on the subsequent purchaser First published in Germany in 2018 in german by amazon.
The manufacturing processes conform to the environmental regulations of the country of origin ISBN 9798438423744 Assistance came from Karen Great Britain and Ashley Canada. Pictures are from Mikos Meininger and Alexander Schaal with Copyright © for both.
Contact: info@11statt12.de

ISBN: 9798438423744
First edition 2022, March

Art can be bought; do it!   **info@11statt12.de**

There is one original (1x), limited art prints (10x each), on acrylic, canvas
or metal with and without frame. Postcards available as a set, too.
Slight colour differences cannot be avoided due to the printing process
and are not covered by the guarantee.

Contact to Mikos Meininger at Kunsthaus Sans Titre in Potsdam/ Germany:
post@sans-titre.de

Where what is:

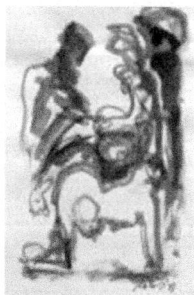

Introduction

Winners of the world! At the top, there is not a lot of room and only one's own greatness counts before oneself. Heroes are like mosquitoes, a plague. As soon as some gold, fame or honour shines, they buzz around. On the other side are the nameless slouchs: Poets without words, not a line they ever put to paper, authors without awork. Colourless painters without brushes, managers without business in any form.

Great words, cuckolded by success, projects sunk at enormous expense, they buzz through executive floors. Unshaken in their faith in themselves. They celebrate their fall! The dimension blows up a defeat only to an unknown height: a fairytale castle that swallows up the budget, so what? But when it's finished, the builder realizes that the foundations won't support it, greatness ensues! A city of millions that turns three functioning airports into none. These are healthy stories of failure, like a balloon without an opening, a barrel without space, a wheel with rough edges.

They lock target groups into cages that do not exist. Neither target nor cage! This not only ruins national economies, but also the entire global economy. It's the bonus that counts. Those who want to see connections should keep their eyes open. He is wrong for the job. Consultants cost more but see less. They encourage the limits of not being able to see into the vicinity of true sagas. Was Homer a hero who failed to arrive or a seeker advised by consultants? The result remains the same.

The purpose of being a boss is: to be a boss! There is and always has been a predecessor, also called a scapegoat. Managers run in orderly circles. The core of a company is the manager. Mars and Pluto orbit around the sun and don't just change orbits on a whim. It is important to consolidate one's own position. Throwing smoke bombs, putting together share packages, scheming, for whom the hour strikes, nothing is unthinkable. A leader is still a leader.

The really big defeats often lie in the small things. We need people with responsibility who believe they are on the right path, even if everyone else thinks it is a wrong path. That is the power of the bummers, in their silence they are louder than those who rant. That is what makes them immortal.

So the opposites are not hero and dead loss or funny and serious. The opposite of a hero is just only not a non-hero, of funny not funny. Both only appear as a team and need each other. Many defeats form the hero and new thoughts are easier to think through laughter. Old thoughts even get a new unexpected sharpness through a joke.

Whether in the Middle Ages as a clown or today on Instagram, stories fulfil a social function, they are the cement of society and teach from childhood. Preferably without pointing fingers. The losers of this world know that their plans fail because of small, as well as big details, every way out is always the beginning of an even bigger disaster. Then categories like good or evil no longer make sense. Any moral unambiguity falls short, always. Those who have learned this are rightly more afraid of the floppers, because a hero simply does not want to be a victim.

Embarrassment is guaranteed in this book. It's for laughs, nothing else.

alexander schaal

stay still
Mikos Meininger 2017

Kick-off

There are jobs - and there are jobs! Acting is one of those: the tension is visible in the face. If there are no scratches, tears, abrasions or other wounds after ninety minutes, i.e., if the actor ends the film with the face of the beginning, the film shows a rather lame ninety minutes. You can always do worse. If it is not only boring, but French, intellectual: ninety minutes of dialogue, two shots, no editing. The main theme is somehow >l'amour<.

Which, as true love, of course remains unattained and unattainable. The leading actress jumps naked through the frame at least once, in slow motion. This underlines the director's intellectual approach. In the brain, the wounds of the viewer heal only slowly. If, on the other hand, the hero's body undergoes an incredible metamorphosis, the film promises suspense. Jason Statham is someone who never ends a film in the same state as he began it.

Neither with his face nor in the physical condition of the beginning. Yes - he is still recognizable, limping into the sunset. However, the ninety minutes gnaw at him, his body, and the nerves of the viewer. That's entertainment, Hartmut thinks.

Hartmut, on the other hand, has one of those other jobs.

He clearly lives more securely as a banker. It is rather his account that jumps and jumps. The cold blows of the overdraft interest, once a month in the pit of his stomach, are certainly comparable to the low blows of a film hero. His current woes would hardly leave Jason Statham cold either: An invitation to the annual conference! With this concluding sentence: clothing appropriate to the occasion. What was that now? Proper clothing, all of his clothes are proper. Only his body often did not fit them anymore.

Above a certain management level, such as head of department, fashion is rarely called slim fit, more fat than fit or rather no fit. The right size was often not in shape, not as fat as obesity. Flab and Fatness were also going on. Or: badly fat. In any case, without shape in every conceivable way. Grey doesn't cover up the excess pounds, but at least it makes you pale and inconspicuous. Or do you know a thin elephant?

On the top floors, the body mass index drops again - here, the work-life balance is more in tune. Adultery keeps you thin, constant fear of being discovered leads to loosing pounds. In addition, the second wife pays more attention to the manager's figure. Attractiveness does not have to be a one-way street. Unobtrusive grey then gives way to shiny grey or fashionable blue, sometimes even with light stripes. Nevertheless, fashion sticks to regular fit. Smokers have the clear advantage of slim lines.

Hartmut, on the other hand, waited for fashion to hit him. So far, that had not been the case. And he looked like it too. By now, his tendency to carelessness just looked rotten.

Even old-clothes containers rejected his donations. There was this point in time when the body no longer played along either. Hartmut had passed it. When? He no longer knew.

Nevertheless, he didn't want to give himself the chance yet. When it came, the fashion, he was there! In concrete terms, that meant that something was always missing. Sometimes a shirt button on the arm, sometimes on the stomach or the collar. Or in all three places. The other day he noticed that his trousers had torn at the pocket. Well, the trousers were eight years old and had been worn since then.

The fact that the dry cleaners suddenly stopped accepting them saddened him. Who was going to judge when clothes were worn out? Hartmut certainly didn't. And now this: ... appropriate to the occasion. Help was needed!

His reservoir of female advice remained meagre, his narrow list contained no one with qualifications apart from his sister and his secretary. Walter he crossed off again, his tennis partner who was completely dressed by his own wife. That was clearly too colorful for Hartmut - even on the tennis court. And Walter's last pair of jeans had several holes and were all pale; supposedly modern. Rather draughty, Hartmut thought. During the lunch break, he sought the proximity of the trainees.

He sat down one table away and watched them closely. He looked like that then, too: The world was still to be conquered, the tie fit only poorly, the suit flapped around the much too thin legs, the shoes more Walmart than bespoke. Hartmut remained true to this style, his colleagues did not. Aubergine and medium green metallic no longer seemed to be current colors, he noticed. So Hartmut no longer owned a wearable suit.

The jacket lining of the blue one was torn. The grey one? These trousers didn't take to the dry cleaners either. Here it was more about the middle main seam: it had parted at the bottom. Body and suit met only partially, but then tautly. Hartmut weighed ten kilos too much for this size. Or more. Back in the office, he instructed his secretary to please make careful enquiries as to what this "appropriate for the occasion" was all about.

His secretary had recently taken to talking on her loud-speaker, sometimes it bothered him, but listening in was better now and Hartmut could finally understand both sides well.

The answers did not calm him down, his attention was on the girlish voice. He heard: >.... try something new ... no more compulsory ties ... like in a start-up ... be modern ... and haha - let's see what the men are hiding under their loose jackets ...< Both women laughed loudly.

Hartmut looked down at himself, without joy. He didn't want to see it, so why should others? And there was no trace of concealment, his belly bulged out clearly. There was no secret! Pale, he sat at the table when his secretary appeared in the door-way. She grasped the situation immediately: >You have nothing in your wardrobe!<

There was the internet now, shopping would be much easi-er and cheaper. Hartmut looked at her with wide eyes. Why he didn't think of it himself - inexplicable. Hartmut spent the next three days shopping on the net. Officially, he revised a project plan that was as good as finished. And you can say something about him, a slippery customer he´s not. His shopping tour was serious and conscientious, good things take time, he got it all in the bag.

Nothing really appealed to him: too wide, too short, too small, not enough grey, until Hartmut came across a site that opened up a new world to him; men's clothing in a package as a package. He ordered three packages: sporty casual for the evening, modern business for the day and casual business for the rest of the meeting. What a day, what excitement.

Hartmut had solved another problem with flying colors, but unfortunately there was no time for rejoicing in public. He would surprise them all. He would be dead smart, fashion would hit him!

Now Hartmut could hardly wait for the meeting, the deadline was approaching. The clothing topic was on everyone's lips; in the tea kitchen, at lunch, in the smokers' corner. Only Hartmut remained cool, so cool that no one expected anything from him. He would arrive lousy as always, an elderly unkempt gentleman in strange colors. Hartmut had long since unpacked the parcels, sorted the shirts by color, neatly folded the trousers and suit jacket, and packed his suitcase for the conference. Even new shoes were included, once soft sporty, once black lace-ups. Chic and very cool, the whole thing!

The meeting then came sooner than expected, like Christmas and birthdays, which do surprise in the end. As an executive, Hartmut had a somewhat larger room. He was happy to have the suitcase brought up. The boy grimaced somewhat disgustedly when he put the suitcase down in the room. And indeed, the suitcase smelled slightly sweet and musty.

When Hartmut opened it, he saw the reason: mould! Maybe he should have taken a newer suitcase after all. He unpacked the things. In many cases, the mould could be knocked off or wiped off the shoes. But the one pair, the sporty shoes, were ruined. One pair of trousers was also riddled with mould, as was a pullover. As a result, Hartmut had a wild mix that he now had to wear: business, casual and sporty. The colors clashed. Fortunately, only a little. Hartmut removed the price tags from the clothes and got dressed. This was stupid now! His perceived clothing size did not correspond to the reality of things.

In order not to damage the clothes, he had deliberately not worn them so far. The grey suit trousers did not close. As a substitute, he could take the light-yellow corduroy trousers. Of the shirts, only the dark pink one remained, and only the light green jacket he could get over his arms - not that it fit, it stretched enormously. He couldn't even get the other jackets on. Of the socks, only the purple ones fit, which looked quite classy with the black shoes, Hartmut thought. He also wore a light brown tie. Hartmut looked at himself in the mirror: different, but not bad. It would only be difficult to bend over, but nobody bends over at a conference.

He stepped out of his room and already the first colleague looked at Hartmut with wide eyes, greeted him and went on. In the lift, his former line manager spoke to him: >Colourblocking, not bad - brave, brave!< And also in the boardroom, after years, he felt that people were seeing him again. Especially women! What a brilliant decision, he couldn't praise himself enough. With difficulty he struggled into the seat, he couldn't expect his trousers to move too much, especially carelessly. A big bang of the trouser button blasting off would be possible at any time.

The meeting started with an innovation. After the management had explained how important the health and well-being of the staff was for the company - healthy eating and abstinence from cigarettes, cigars and co - a nutritionist explained healthy eating. That would really ban such a conference, Hartmut thought. This tendency was new to him. Hot Dogs in the canteen was probably out. What a pity! After the woman, an over-motivated young man jumped onto the stage and jumped, dancing up and down with his legs the whole time while he spoke. He shouted: >Stand up! Push the chairs away! Make some space around you!< And everyone joined in. Cruelly. Hartmut had no choice, he too stood up and pushed his chair slightly backwards. >Let's go! Something easy to start with. Ten little squats!<

At Hartmut's first implied movement, a loud pop hissed through the room. He suddenly felt very free around his bottom. But what hero ever finishes his session the way he started it.

And yes, it was all there to see: Hartmut the Jason Statham of his company.

stay down
Mikos Meininger 2017

Assumed

>Is colleague Bruns cheating now? Does he Play around or not?< the question saved the lunch table from embarrassing silence. Hush, everyone at the table was listening. Richard Schneider looked around the table. Eye to eye, he´s back in business.

>Bruns is cheating?< asked Mrs Müller.

>I don't know, I'm just asking!< said Schneider.

>I can't imagine it< said Mrs Müller.

>I can!" whispered Meier. Meier could imagine anything. Always. Only it´s dirty and that´s not to small.

>With whom then?< asked Mrs Müller.

Now speaking normally Meier replied: >In this position you can always find someone. What about the young chickens who are now in training? He's a big fish.<

Richard Schneider leaned back, listening to the discussion. More and more excitedly and headvenly, the lunch colleagues discussed the sins of Herrmann Bruns, their line-manager for years. After ten minutes there was unanimity at the table, there was something. The agreement was: Bruns was concealing a flirt. Or more. Good, but not good enough. They had uncovered it, they had discovered the jungle of Bruns secrets.

It took three hours for the news to reach Bruns himself. Or better, lying in the arms of his secretary. The message, not himself.

His secrecy could kept a secret, in this case for five minutes, then she had to ask her boss personally. She entered the office with a seemingly urgent memo. While Bruns read the letter, his secretary looked at him closely. A man of upper age, always elegantly dressed, but not attractive. Nose hairs and ear hairs were visible, the haircut rather short than practical or even modern.

>What are you looking at me like that?< Herrmann Bruns asked his secretary. >Nothing< she said.

Bruns looked sternly and said gruffly: >But you are bright red in the face. You only turn that way when you are infinitely embarrassed. So what is it?<

At first she was silent, but then it burst out: >There is the talk in town that you are having an affaire.<

Bruns was silent, thinking. But instead of losing color, as she had expected, his face remained completely normal. Then he laughed: >With whom?< He looked at his secretary: >You know my schedule best. When is there time for that? And look at me - as a woman, do you find anything attractive?<

Now his secretary was really blushing, her head was on fire. >There you go!< Bruns said. >You answered it yourself!< He was still looking at her: >Who is spreading this gross nonsense?<

>Supposeling the gang around Schneider. But of course, I don't know details!< she said.

>Could you tell me with whom I ´m going around? I hope it's at least a woman.<

>Something younger, a twenty something or so – a student, maybe?<

>Thank you!<

Shortly before closing time, Herrmann Bruns roamed the office corridors. A black-haired girl, one of the trainees, was holding his hand. Hand by hand, they walked into the office where the lunch table sat. They strolled from desk to desk and left the office without saying one word.

>I knew it!< Mrs Müller whispered at room volume.

Then Bruns stuck his head through the door again: >Mr Schneider, we both have an appointment tomorrow at 7.30 a.m. In my office!<

Bruns left an awkwardly silent office until closing time. Without a word or a greeting, one after the other disappeared. Only Richard Schneider stayed longer today. Maybe he could catch Bruns before he left. But Bruns' secretary told him that he was already away today with his niece. An out-of-office appointment. His niece! Schneider ran his fingers between his hair. Shit, shit, shit. And how did Bruns know it came from him? What had he done. Except, he hadn't said anything, just asked! The others had suspected Bruns. Exactly: the others! He was innocent as a baby. Just a simple question. No less, no more. That´s it!had suspected Bruns. Exactly: the others! He was innocent as a baby. Just a simple question. No less, no more. That´s it!

Despite this prepared line of defense, Schneider could not sleep. At seven he sat at his desk, at 7.20 Bruns secretary informed him that he was prevented from attending today. The appointment would be postponed til tomorrow.

At eight, the colleagues arrived one by one, everyone looked quiet at Schneider. The fact that he was still there meant nothing. At the breakfast break the first questions were: >How was it this morning?< >Was it very bad?< The news that Schneider's appointment with Bruns had been postponed to the next day gone from door to door. No, they are running!

>There is more traffic here today, than on times square.< Mrs Müller remarked when the fourth mate stuck his head through the door to say *how are you*. Richard Schneider, on the other hand, did without lunch today. His presence in the cafeteria was complete, in the table conversations and overall. As Audrey Hepburn put it so well: If you want to be the centre of the party, don't go.

By afternoon, the interest on Schneider died, new topics took first places on the top ten of the gossip scale. Only

Schneider sat rigidly at his desk, there was no thought of work. And he didn't sleep a wink the second night either, leaving his bed extremely unrelaxed.

In the morning he sat in Bruns office and waited. The boss was coming in no time, his secretary said. Bruns arrived around eight or so. Not necessarily on time today. Ten minutes later, Bruns received him. Schneider was sweating with excitement, his face looked old and grey.

>Morning, Mr Schneider.<

>Good morning, Mr Bruns. You wanted to see me?<

>Oh yes< Bruns scratched his chin: >What was that all about? Oh, now I remember, just a rumor. It doesn't matter. We shouldn't talk about rumors? Isn't it? It brings them to life! Pointless and wasteful was that< Bruns stood up and accompanied Schneider to the door: >Thank you for coming!<

Pale, Schneider crept to his desk. He said nothing all day, talked to no one. In the evening he left early.

>Is he dismissed or not?< asked Mrs Müller.

>Dismissed? I don't know. He looked bad in any case. It´s a warning notice?< said colleague Meier.

>I'm just asking!< Mrs Müller added. And raised her pointer as a warning.

>Or is he ill?< asked Meier. Everyone was silent. >Maybe cancer! He smokes too< suggested Mrs Müller. >And not a little< said Meier. >At least three packs!< >In the morning! < Everyone laughed.

And so, the rumor >Schneider has cancer< left her room and flitted across the hall - from office to office! By the way to Bruns' secretary ...

stay silent
Mikos Meininger 2017

My wish for you is small, but not easy. Please do not judge me too quickly. Above all, make your judgement only after you have heard my story. Others have already judged me.

Yes, I killed my husband. I wonder if he really had to die. I feel so much better now and so does almost everyone else. He wasn't a monster, not physically. He didn't beat me, rape me or harass me. It was his words that hit me, that hurt me. Yes, just words.

Murder is also just a horrible word! It was more: I severed the tie between us. No one suspects what lies behind it! The years full of torment; how small I felt, how useless I felt and no sign of hope. No one anywhere who could or wanted to save me.

Stop! Maybe you're getting the wrong impression after all. Yes, I married him more than twenty years ago. For love. As it should be in the best case. We met at vocational school. And yes, he was by far the best catch to be had. Why he chose me, everyone wondered - me too. But I enjoyed it: this tall slender handsome man. Dark short hair, shoulders like a cross, the perfect triangle: strong shoulders, narrow hips, big love. No - hot love. And perfect to lean on.

I had arrived at the big harbour of a small family. Kids, a house, a garden, we wanted the whole nine yards. Never had a man been so tender, sensitive and yet so passionate with me. I was floating on a cloud, cushing everything. Reality has always been hard to reach, even my parents accused me of that. However, this time I didn't even let her in.

First our neighbour spoke to me. She asked me if my husband really had to be away every weekend. That was two years after our wedding and I hadn't even noticed it until then.

We had both settled into our lives. This included my weekends off, which I enjoyed very much. While other couples argued about shopping, I could do all our shopping on Saturday alone and at leisure. On Sunday, I would cook one or two dishes in advance, in case he was late, a meeting lasted longer, and I was already in bed and asleep. Then he could at least put something in the microwave in the evening and didn't have to come to bed starving. He praised my cooking and always ate everything. When I told him about the encounter with the neighbour and laughed out loud, he got all red in the face. I had never seen him so angry.

Something must have happened afterwards. The contact with the neighbour had never been intense, yet now it had broken off. When she met me on the street, she changed sides. I don't think we ever spoke again. How could we? I didn't have any more time!

>Haven't you always wanted to have a garden? Not this puddle here, a real one?< he asked me a few weeks later. Of course I wanted one! As if he could read my mind. Finally my own garden, my own pond, a beloved retreat full of romance.

He even had a proposal already. He had found a house on the other side of town, with an English garden. The house as enchanting as the former owners. I could already see during the viewing how we could both grow old here and enjoy our twilight years.

On the veranda, on a swing, with a view of the pond: us in our little world. It was hardly real, it was so beautiful. Indeed, we bought this house. I was able to move in immediately.

He took care of everything; I didn't have to do anything. What a treasure! I couldn't believe my luck and my love became all the stronger and deeper. Now I was completely blind. The next few years flew by in my floral frenzy. Twice our garden was awarded as the most beautiful in the whole neighbourhood. Unfortunately, he didn't really notice. By now it was not only the weekends, but almost all days of the year when he was not at home – or in modern 24/7/365 a year! There was even a rumor in the neighbourhood that I was a widow, and my husband was my brother, who only took care of me occasionally.

>Oh, he lives here?< the newspaper seller asked me once. >I thought he lived at the other end of town.< I looked at her confused: >What makes you think that?< >I once helped out in a newspaper shop there. He came every day.< >Yes< I said.

>We used to live there. But it's been years.< >I'm talking about last month.< said the newspaper woman, destroying my mood. She was wrong, that much was certain. And that was all I wanted to know.

Strangers! Always they wanted to destroy the happiness of others. I had enough for the day, I went to my pond. But my mind kept working, the thoughts wouldn't go away. And suddenly I found myself in the study, not at the pond. I rummaged through our files, which I usually never bother with, but everything looked unsuspicious. What a stupid cow I was, what I let myself think. I was ashamed. When I got up, I saw a piece of paper, it was pink. I pulled it out of the pile; the kiss on it was not mine. I wiped my finger across my mouth: lipstick! I went to bed early and put a plate in the microwave.

The next day I bought another newspaper. This time I asked a few questions, and the newspaper woman was only too happy to answer. She said that my reaction yesterday had also seemed strange to her and that she had called the shop.

Yes, he still came there often to buy the paper. Almost every day. The selection of newspapers was also right. Those were his favorite papers. >Oh, I see< said the newspaper saleswoman >the yellow press times is still there too.< It is often only small, soft words that bring down great walls.

No man read the yellow press times: heart and pain, made-up news from the European royal houses all over the world. My husband hated it. When I bought it once, he went completely mad: >You too! I see this trash every day in the office. Even the marketing manager reads this crap.<

I remembered that so well because until then I hadn't known that there was a marketing manager. Until then, he always spoke of a marketing manager. Who also knew no weekends and who made business trips so relentlessly bland? So now, another woman.

Jealousy doesn't suit me. I never wanted to be such a mother hen. But knowing and doing are never the same thing. I found myself in the garden growing two herbs for the first time that looked beautiful and were wonderfully poisonous. The blue rocket, aconitumnapellus, a color wonder of blue, changing tone in the middle of the flower, to a white blob; everything about it is poisonous! Warriors and hunters liked to rub their arrowheads with it; less than five mg is enough for respiratory distress, cardiac arrest. But the most beautiful thing about it: all without external symptoms. Drinking is enough!

As a murder weapon, it has a dubiously gruesome, brutal reputation. For a herbal poison, it's downright cosmopolitan. Now what goes better with blue than purple? Daphne mezereum, a common daphne! The golden saxifrage looks so wonderfully innocent in the hedge. Like a sweetly opened snapdragon. Everything about the daphne is poisonous too. But its chastity is not pure. It is even better than respiratory distress and cardiac arrest: poisoning creeps in.

First there is a burning and tingling sensation in the mouth, then the lips and part of the face swell up. Hoarseness follows, then swallowing becomes difficult. In the climax, the poisoning tends to cause pain, cramps and diarrhoea. Then comes the finale: the circulation fails. The lethal dose is a mere twelve berries! When both were ripe and ready for harvesting, I plucked them out; angry at myself. He was the love of my life, we would be able to sort it out. I was ashamed of my thoughts, my plans. What a disgusting person I was! I asked for a date, a weekend together. Not at home. At the seaside. And he agreed.

Astonished, but nevertheless he agreed. A big hotel, five houses with a wellness area. I should have a good time. He had already planned a lot of the time for me: Ayurveda, relaxing with hot stones, active massage, autogenic training in hot mud and Friday night candlelight dinner. What an attentive man! Saturday, I needed him, I said. All his attention, for one day. We would have to talk.

He nodded his understanding and booked a table away from the hustle and bustle. And we talked: I showed him the pink paper, told him about the newspaper woman, his usual choices and asked questions. His face color changed from red to grey to pink to green and grey again, in the end it was green like lime - he really could explain everything.

My husband, so sweet, so well-behaved and understanding. I could hardly look him in the eye in the evening, I had such a guilty conscience. We went to our room drunk. That evening I got pregnant!

My head was pounding, the whole of the next morning was like a slow-moving love movie played out in slow motion. He hadn't been in bed for two or three hours; I snuggled into his pillow, which smelled so wonderfully of him. I ordered breakfast and skipped the first two wellness appointments. Slowly my head cleared up. My thoughts sorted themselves out and my guilty conscience returned. Wearing only my bathrobe and otherwise completely free, I sat down on the balcony and enjoyed the beach.

Sip by sip, I sipped my coffee. Until my cup fell out of my hand: there sat my husband, embracing another woman. They were kissing and stroking each other's faces in love. Was it him or was I still drunk? I needed binoculars. There was one in the room, I got it, looked for the couple. They were gone!

Maybe I had mistaken him for someone else. I took my mobile phone and called him. I could hardly hear him, the wind was so loud: >Where are you? I miss you so much< I asked. >I'm jogging on the beach< he said. >Aren't you at the massage?< >No< I answered. >Oh...< he said, sounding scared and hollow. >Then I'll come as soon as I can, dear.<

And he came to the room after half an hour - surprisingly dry for his jogging. Whereas he was usually sweating after one step, like a high-performance athlete.

I showed him the spot where I had seen him. He laughed: >Still not enough?< Then he turned around. >I'm starting to worry, I don't want it to become manic.< And we both laughed.

The rest of the weekend was wonderful. Six weeks later, I knew I was pregnant. I had never seen him so pale. But we celebrated, we went out to eat, we drank. >One or two sips, it doesn't do anything< he said. But it did! Two months later, the gynaecologist advised us to terminate the pregnancy. The brain fold was not growing together properly. The doctor asked me if I was an alcoholic. I said no, I was sick to my stomach.

No child! An unfulfilled wish, my unfulfilled wish. What fools we were. We should have known; we had killed our baby. In any case, he was less upset than I was. After I had an abortion, his mood visibly rose. Maybe we were just too young to have a child.

One evening, my husband was away on business again, a suppressed number called my mobile. I answered it. A child's voice asked: >Papa?< A boy. In the background I heard a man's voice say: >What do you think you're doing, give me back my mobile phone!< And the connection was interrupted. I couldn't call back, but I didn't have to. I knew who had called. My child had got another one. His voice remained in my ear, the boy's and my husband's.

Being blind is a way to live a happy life; only at some point reality demands its due. Blindness becomes stupidity.

I felt bad, so cheated, so useless, so betrayed. I couldn't even say what it was exactly. But I felt bad every day. Nauseous after getting up, nauseous after coffee, nauseous after lunch and even more nauseous in the evening. He didn't even notice, as he was only home once or twice a month.

He also didn't notice that I lost ten kilos. When did we talk to each other? One evening he looked into the garden, turned around and said: >The garden is so beautiful this year. It's dominated by blue and purple. A dream of purple and blue!< Yes, he was right.

We didn't see each other at all during the summer. He was always on the go, had to go to Nice, to Barcelona, to Rome. He was getting browner and browner, the company was expanding. He was indispensable. That summer, I turned pure white. I was so pale that my blood veins shimmered blue through my skin. I'm afraid I looked a little creepy. A fact that did not sit well with me in court. There is little sympathy for a living corpse.

Then came autumn, I harvested my garden, made compote, jam, liqueur. And, yes. Yes, this year I also harvested both blue herbs. A book called >Alternative Remedies< had been on my dessert table for two years. I had no secrets: dry, mortar, powder, collect. How does it dissolve? Good in water, good in milk; nothing settles if it stands for a few hours. Perfect! I was ready. And now?

Later, everyone accused me of being a black widow. That I had a cunning plan. In reality, I was quite clueless. How could I use the powder, how to give it to my husband? Would I even be able to give it to him? Did I want him to die? No, that's exactly what I didn't want. I wanted to live happily with him.

Nothing more, nothing less. Only he screwed it up, ruined our lives. Lived without me. So I took a soda bottle, poured the whole crop into it. Must have been over 50 mg of powder. Put the bottle next to the fridge. And forgot about it.

I also forgot that he wanted to be home the next weekend. On Sunday, as I was peeling potatoes in the kitchen, lost in my thoughts, something held me from behind. I pushed it away and turned around with my knife at the ready.

There he stood: eyes wide, mouth contorted in terror. But then he laughed, laughed at me. He picked up the bottle next to the fridge, his mouth twisted contemptuously. >You're too stupid even to kill me.< he muttered and drank the lemonade.

stay safe
Mikos Meininger 2017

Evening Event

Sixty euros was the limit. It was not allowed to cost more. Dirk shook his head inwardly, where was the fun in that?

Outwardly, he raised his head like his glass: >What a solemn moment in these gloomy days. Cheers!< >Hear, hear< it resounded through the room< glasses clinked. The crowd drank, some sipped conscientiously.

>This white wine from Franconia is first class< >That's what I call an excellent wine!< Dirk looked at his neighbours in amazement. >This Cuvée first!< >Yes, yes, enjoyment can be so simple.< >It's a miracle that this slightly spicy-floral, with fragrant stone fruit notes on the palate not only suggests freshness, but also tastes of crystal-clear fruit.< >So, so.< said Dirk's neighbour. The waitress poured more. >Me too, me too!< the other person sitting next to him stretched his glass and his neck upwards. There was wine, women; - the only thing missing was singing.

>Mine is cultivated in the area around Heidelberg, while in the glass it is still fighting a contest of fruit and vegetation, on the palate it unfolds a mixture of herb meadow and young pineapple against grapefruit.< >An interesting combination!< >Isn´t?< >Such a wine never moves only on one level, sometimes the aroma stretches into the foreground.< Dirk was amazed, these two colleagues were usually silent during the entire conference and now they were classifying the wines, like professionals.

On the other hand, Dirk heard: >I have a soft spot for whimsical wines.< >Oh?< >At home I have a Pinot Noir, for ten euros. It comes with all its heart, shows its broadside full of cherries and dark berries. Then it's tart like a chestnut, then come the slightly balsamic notes: Tobacco and such. With underlying acidity.< >Oh, yes?< >It's a totally balanced wine. A hearty price-pleasure ratio!< They laugh. The men from the Oh´s turns to the waiter: >Do you have a Burgundy?<

Of course there is a Burgundy. He tests, drinks and sips: >All Burgundies are colourful in the evening!< They both laugh again. >The first sip is the best.< Both nod steadily. >All colors will agree in the dark!< >It is, it is!< Comfortable communion sets in. >See how the wine streaks forms?< >Wonderful!< >A very noble grape!< >How does it taste?< >It's pure fruit: pear, ripe peach, pomelo.< >White or red peach?< >More like white.< >It sounds quite delightful.< >Yes, it is, isn´t it?< Both are silent. >The bouquet quotes stone fruit, hay and wet stone very lightly.< >And tangerine!< >Yes, exactly, tangerine, now that you mention it. On the palate, a racy acidity with mineral, slightly stiff texture.< >Like tree bark?< >No, more like jeans.< >Stonewashed?< >Yes, exactly!<

Opposite, Dirk hears: >A quite pleasing mouthfeel, rather soft with delicate melting.< >Yes, that's true. Only the alcohol is poorly integrated.< >Not true?< Dirk is amazed. The whole group talks and revels in the wine. During each of the last entire meetings he could count the word contributions on one hand

and now this. Dirk was amazed, also at the wine consumption. It was not allowed to be more than sixty euros per person. That was a new internal guideline.

>Murderously good this wine!< Dirk said to his right, they were at the next bottle. >Wood barrel, palatable wood barrel.< >Despite that, juicy, not such a bulky wood tone, rather roasted and nutty aromas.< >A bit of sauerkraut, a bit of wild berries are also in play.< >Limestone-mineral and yet a fine acidity in the tannin structure. It could be a little more elegant.< >It can tast it< >Tastes good, yes!<

Dirk saw the Green Veltiner in front of him. He read the label: grape vine and Sauvignon blanc were also mixed in. Wine was always a risky purchase! You never knew what to expect. The corked unknown quickly became a corked evening if the plonk didn't taste good. Dirk poured himself a glass. He drank away his dilemma, the taste buds reacted positively at first. But visually, the wine was a washout.

>What is it like?< asked his neighbour. >I taste asphalt with borite, freshly tarred country road with lime residue from marble quarrying. The benzene only comes to the fore at the back of the tongue. But the side wings taste the 6-cylinder: soot without remorse!< By now the whole table was silent. Everyone was looking at Dirk. He was the line manager. He was a philistine. Everyone smiled indulgently. Only Dirk didn't know why. Irritated, he got up and went to wash his hands.

At the table, the conversation picked up again. >What a creep!< >You bet!< >Awful.< >No culture.< >I bet he's an East German!< >Worse, much worse, very little plait. A country bumpkin. Moren!< >That says it all.< A table neighbour took the wine bottle from Dirk, poured himself a big gulp and drank greedily. His face turned first red than white. >And?< >What kind of swill!< >What does it taste like?< >Petrol, diesel, disgusting!< >What do you know!< >Taste it for yourself!<

Dirk went from the toilet straight to the waiter, gave him ten Euros: >Thank you, that will curb their drinking zeal.< >Who drinks methylated spirits voluntarily!< Both nodded to each other, conspiracy forms a strong bond between people. Dirk went to bed with the certainty that he would not need the sixty euros per person. He was satisfied with this evening event.

stay here
Mikos Meininger 2017

Are you a part of the company or not? A part of the solution or rather the stumbling block? Are you inside the company's information or more outside? These questions are really important, or better: the answers are, aren't they? For you and your career leader. Is your name in an e-mail by the field to: or cc: and which is better? Don't say: it depends. Nothings depends on if the career path is clogged with colleagues. A lot of questions and Bob can't answer them. Where people are, there is talk, often small talk. Rarely deep. Bob Muller, lead-writer of the Yam-Group found his very own way, step by step. Now he writes the answers for the big fish in the company, and sometimes for the General Manager, too.

The new product of the group was a very dysfunctional hoover, electric and loud as a plane taking off. A perfect mix from white and brown goods, more washing machine or refrigerator than hoover and more home entertainment, too. Just like any mixture of things, the hoover don't work in every kind of tasks. The construction unit was completely play it by ear for design and function. And yes, it doesn't work. The vacuum cleaner had a camera and wifi, could answer twitter and send notes. Only he is little weak in the chest when it comes to sucking dirty things. His real task. Actually, it was supposed to be an ice cream maker. The Yam-Group toyed with the idea and decided against it. Then there were a lot of changing line managers, changing goals and a lack of money for the project. A weak engine and too loud for everything, so only the hoover remained. Old things make profit, a lot of old things rake it in more money.

Never before had the company received such a large number of complaints. Bob paid these things no attention, as wasn't his work. The normal response came from other units, all have a *customer* in their words, as customers-happiness, customers-well-being or count-customers-oneself lucky. Yet the company was in the public eye, competent support was wanted. A monumental answer came from Bob, he writes this in under a half hour:

Dear Sirs,

It's so nice to hear from you and our journey is now just beginning. The Yam-Groups aggregate further single premium hoover shall be apportioned equally among the existing Policies and consequently in relation and relationship to each such Policy the Further Minimum Sum Assured secured by the part of the aid and said aggregate further Minimum Sum Assured specified in the Schedule divided by the total number of the existing Policies further Participating Sum Assured so secured shall be a sum equal to the aggregate Further Participating Sum Assured so specified by total number of further single paid existing single premium Policies. You be a part of us.... It's our pleasure, to see your enjoyment with this device. Let us learn and know more about our partnership with best products from the Yam-Group. You are now a Yam, too.

With best wishes

It´s worked generally. No further questions, no further complaints. Bob knows his job. When his boss asked him for a meeting, he expected only praise. However, what he got was an hour of shouting. His spirits were down. He doesn't suggest it. What was wrong with his letter? First and foremost, it was the appellant: Sir Rob. On the follow up list of her queen he was number two thousand fourthy no aged one! Lessons from pandemic was learned, how fast could thousands of people die. And there are always pandemic times. Once thought: HIV, Sars, swineflu, Covid. The door is always open for anything new. Sir Robert wasn´t the biggest cat under all fat cats, though he was smaller than a leopard and bigger than a normal street cat. His face was glowing as a chili when he, every replied to everything with a whiplash-inducing response, words keen and sharp. This Mail was the reason for Bobs nasty encounter with his line manager. Bob is in the line of fire.

Bob´s hope was, somehow, someway, he ´ll gone get out here. It was just a whole lot of pretty in a whole lot of crazy. But his boss saved the best for last. And at this point they were not done yet. > Only for the record, this is exactly what I was concerned about<, the line manager said: > It's a *need to know for you*, and all you need to know is *you* work for me! Did they warn you about me? If my influence looks like as a rice grain for you, I swear, it's more powerful as a hand grenade.< Both keep quiet. After a while Bob said: >We aren´t in clover there is to much whistle in the dark. I´m having kittens about all this. I'm not judging. I've buried a lot of mistakes in my life, too. The worst part of it is, they're going to blame us for the whole thing! A solution could be to tell everybody everything.< His boss looking at him stunned: >Are you off your meds?< Bob swallowed hard. It´s going on: >Was this like a, uh, pep talk? Yes? That was a pep talk, management gold standard, it´s all easy peasy with us, like a walk in the park? Won't fit anymore?< Bob came in mind, he had perhaps slightly misjudged the situation. A half hour of tightrope-walking is a big undertaking and although the will to succeed was undoubtedly there, Bob has seen promising starts descend into simple revenge operations against the closest staff. Fingers crossed for himself, that it will not come to this, he thought. Everything is a little more on the nose than it might ideally be. Bob gets a control issue, hysterical he´s rubbing on the table in front of him at the ring left by a drink set down without a coaster.

>There is no w in you, YOU´re in no position to make any ideas or demands.< the line manager faltered: > Don't get high-spirited on me and ruin a good thing, you aren't the kind of person who can get the answers. And if you can´t get those answer, your head will be on a pike. Only yours!< He nodded to himself: > You believe in leadership? Better believe in leverage!< Bob preferred to remain silent. >And pressure on you will come! A phone call with friends can change everything. The tabloids are pleasure doing business with me and they call me, Captain Newsmaker! Figure this out, how uncomfortable it can be between the lines or

as a headline, too. Bob though, if his line manager will be feeding the lions, he should urgently go to clear his browser history. It would be appropriate. Bob felt what will happen when the sun runs out of fuel. He wasn't even a white dwarf in the Milky Way with faint light, he was ground based, and he made a mistake. Indeed, he was too old for this, though not old enough for that had happened yet. >There isn't a setting on the dryer: Normal. We are getting people to act against their own self-interest, they bought crap. Junk and we earn a lot of money. That's our business! Now you got personal. You're focus wasn't on boldly going where few have gone before. You will be visiting the fat cat. And fix it!< Bob snatched at air. >You got something better to do?< asked his line-manager.

When Bob went back to his office, he thought of this song, he saw the old man in the streets of London in the closed down market kicking up the papers with his worn-out shoes, no pride in his eyes, lonely, need whom to lead himself, dirt in his hair and clothes, sitting at a quarter past eleven near a café and wanders alone far away from a home. Bob never felt closer to this man, and how could people say that the sun shine or it's easy to change your mind. The cards are on the table. Although Bob had expected to be sacked in this call. And he's just poised now to lead over these things. The true, ugly face of his line-manager is now being seen by different victims and Bob was the elephant in the room. Quick to dismiss for the rest of the company without consequences. Levelling up my arse, it's meaningless, this company is going backwards at a rate of knots, a two-tier society: Big Fish and Fat Cats. If you were not one of them two, it´s just to gauge how terribly disadvantaged you are. The list of self-created scape-goats by this company, to use as 'human shields' for self-protection is deplorable though Bob. Only that did not help either.

>There's nothing like a vacation to make you appreciate home.< he said as he sat at his desk at home again. And his head started to work. He knows, he´s playing with fire. Now, he thinks, it´s better if he´s fighting fire with fire. However, he´s not going to pitch him that. Overall, there was only one rule: No money, no honey. Bob knows he wasn´t a dickhead for himself. Everyone has a weakness. And a weakness can be leveraged. What was these from Sir Rob?

The phone call sobered him as a normal drinker in first January weeks every year. Nausea and headaches included, is getting out of hand in the first minute. Sir Rob wasn´t the expected load mouth, he was in a very special kind much worse. Whose ego could fill a room, just a fat cat. The whole britishness of centuries lay in his voice. A noblesse of doing nothing for a lazy life, as solid as an oak cupboard, dignified and old. Only old, not rich or anything else. His voice smelled of an aged scent with a lot of upper class and aristocracy. It was more an illusion of a greatness than reality. His accentuation of the syllables was rather beyond, hard, toneless, dick e crunky and of course spoken with a pointed nos. Strange phone signals are coming from him, the centre of his highness.

Bob wasn´t sure what is emitting of them. Like some old buildings where you weren't clear, was it a little joke from the master builder or wasn´t built in one day. Only if cash present and they loaf a skimpy with their working time. Bob will wonder when it all stops, it won't: >Listen, I can keep a secret, okay? What do you give me?< asked Sir Rob without any shyness. Bob feels that Sir Rob offering peanuts to him and pouring boiling oil on below on the same time, while he pulls up the rescue ladder. The voice also smelled of old lords, the thoughts betrayed the modern crook.

Bob saw not Sir Rob. He had the eyes of a naked mole rat and the hearing of an unaddressed dog. He lived in the body of a centenarian. At fifty! His early years as a punk took their toll. Unclear what the reason was, if it was the heroin, LSD or just the boozing. Who knows and Bobs interest was even less? Anyway, for a fat cat this plays no matter, where the reproductive partners consist only of nephews and nieces, Sir Rob restricted this only to direct descendants of the Celts. He retained his aversion to all new strangers, even in his sexual preferences.

It was clearly evident that neither Bob nor Sir Rob had no strategic plan for this call. Bob was glad that his business leader aren´t waking up to this harsh reality. In this respect this phone speech was indeed a triumph, he has managed in universal disorientation the faults of the hoover. A real triumph this time. Sickening though. And far away from close to the end. Only in the end for an offer Bob was useless, clueless and hapless. He was hopeless over a situation created from Sir Rob and he didn´t understand what he expected. In such situations he was free of any imagination or creativity, without any trouble for himself. He makes up his mind. Things get complicated now, he was always fearful of the pink slip from his line manager and looking like a drowned rat.

>Let´s face it!< he heard himself saying and Sir Rob got going: > Don't worry about the insignificant details and don't sweat the small stuff - focus on the big picture!< Bobs knows what is it to do, now, but Beggars can´t be choosers. It was clear. Sir Rob continued with his speech: >Can you imagine the furor and din of indignation that would erupt from the tabloid's media machine if blue blood is deliberately deceived. I will see a national crisis, it could be howls of outrage accompanied by a baying for blood and a clamour for heads on platters. This hoover is a great conspiracy against humanity, a dereliction of duty, in the UK exists a hierarchy of tolerance, which corresponds to an individual's background and place in society. Yes, it´s a hypocrisy. However it´s better for you if you are not in the eye of the hurricane, in the middle of non-acceptable conduct of your company.< Bob nodded, this was true. This noble toad he had to swallow before it ate

him up: >With all respect Sir Rob, I can´t deliver, if my troops are disaffected. As soon as I know exactly what you want I will keep the troops in line.< >Hear, hear!< answered Sir Rob: >I´m over well. You will keep your bacon and I will be rich.< Now, Bob was back in business, in his philosophy everybody could be valuable. Even a selfish total failure like Sir Rob. >What do you thing about, if we both walk together the digital highway?< Sir Rob didn't think it was bad at all, too. Any sufficiently advanced technology is indistinguishable from magic, thought Bob and magic he would really need with him. If Bob could take care, he will get him a spot in the list of world wide web in the next four weeks. Sir Rob owned everything a growing up buddy needs: drugs experience, tactless behavior and endless greed. Welcome to the world of pubescent men.

>Did you hear from facebook before?< asked Bob. Sir Rob mumbled to himself: >Oh, antisocial networks.< Bob did not find this objection bad at all. >However, facebook is only for old people. I am not over the hill yet. Let's take something younger.< said Sir Rob. And Bob found, he dealt a good hand. However always it failed in the end on Sir Rob. This was wrong or other things did not go at all. Bob started the next conversation with >What kept you this time?< Sir Rob was visibly outraged by this opening. Bob wasn´t yet at the end. After several days and what felt like more than a hundred suggestions: >I agreed to help out, but not so. You can sit around on your fuckin' arse. Thanks to your incompetence, our plan is utterly ruined.< This language Sir

Rob understood: >You're reacting badly to some bad news.<
Both were silent. >I didn't think you had the balls, man< said Sir
Rob >You're a fucking lunatic, you know that? Do you find
something funny? Your business is your own. And I´m in my
field. Finally let me do my job!< Sir Rob answered: >Just take
some time!< >My mind is clear. What you talking about?< Sir
Rob puffed scornfully: >Once you start, there is no going back.
Is a one-way street. I mean, everything in the net is traceable.
Nothing disappears. That is a risk. This kind of job doesn't come
with a receipt.< Bob mulls it over now, cold feet: >I told you it's
covered. And our rate's an even one. Is that sort of cash just lying
around? We're talking about a figure so close to 300.000 in a
week we might as well call it that. Uncertainty is part of it and
quality always costs. Even when it is time!< >So as your hoover?
< >Watch your mouth! So are we on?< Bob asked. Yes, they
were in business, in the end.

But even the best planning can go wrong when reality calls.
Nothing happened in the first few weeks, then even less. Four
likes and two followers, more by accident than intentionally. That
was nothing. Sir Rob wasn´t the next viral star on the internet,
rather a glow worm. Bob thought, success on the internet has
nothing to do with real life. Powerful people had better disguise
themselves as jokers, because their power is worth nothing on the
net. Even they lose it in no time. Underdogs roam cunningly
through the paths of the system. No big fish would like to be a
flop or a no-hoper, in real life or in the web-world. And certainly

not a fat cat. You can´t fix both. Those who want dignity should avoid social networks, everything is nothing on the net. The king becomes a clown so quickly that he doesn't even notice. Light up for a bad death. The internet staff cancel their request so quickly as soon as lost the desire of everything, it´s all marketing for seconds and every message has the same value, whether an earthquake, a royal wedding or a cat image. Create attention, nippy and sharply, without regard for loss. Those who don't understand this don't deserve any sympathy either, because the managers behind them have long since made a living out of it.

Bob went through the most important topics again and again. Cats, Sir Rob was allergic about them. Sex, Sir Robs' preference for little boys did not please Bob at all. Even if it did not seem out of character for aristocrats or priests. Drugs, Bob didn't want to do that to the Yam-Group, or to himself. And when they said Sir Rob is too much to drink, so he isn´t to short of his sexual orientation. Anyway, Rock´n Roll, never Sir Rob was further away from it, even for Punk it was no longer enough. Healthy Life, Bob had to laugh at himself. That´s all was bad enough and it was shocking if Bob was confronted with this real lack of ideas paired or better coupled with not being able at all. In her next call Bob asked: >We need a friend in high places. Do you have acquaintances who are known by name and rank?<

And it works. Different than expected, however it was incredible. A close relative with the name Harry made a comment under Sir Robs profile. A blogger mistook this for a more famous

Harry. And then it went off. More than one million followers in a month and Sir Rob earning a lot of money every week. He was now the face of the hoover and shows all the dysfunctional things. Funny, ironic and with a smile on his lips. There couldn't have been better advertising. People snatched the hoover out of the company's hands. Everyone could be happy and content. Only Bob had to see his boss again. He suspected it was about something bad.

It began quite harmlessly: >Come inside, Bob, Come on.< Bob knows a watched pot never boils. He remained kind of calm and will only deliver the goods. >The chickens are coming home to roost ...< his line-manager laughed: >... or is the henhouse Sir Rob without confusion now? Even if I see the users I was in fuzzy flashback as a reminder how bad it´s all began. Now we grow up rapidly and it´s looking all exotic and not gripping for me. I'm only just over halfway through the current vids as a slave of my own job I had not more time for these things, even it seems to go down very well, isn´t it?< Bob stayed formal: >Of Course, just in general terms, that goes without saying. I put a bit of stick about, then I make him jump. And I shall absolutely be loyal to the Yam-Group and to you as my line-manager.< >Yes, yes. I know.< his boss suddenly seemed distracted: >Nothing lasts forever. Even the longest, the most glittering reign must come to an end someday. However not on my watch, you understand? Are we ready for these things?< > People aren´t asking questions about Sir Rob< said Bob, without him knowing what it was about. >Good, good. We can't have it that he throw one´s weight around. Do not forget, this bastard came from high places.< >Could this the *Sir* in his name means?< >No jokes Bob, no jokes!<

Sir Rob played in his league, he calls Baroness Sophie of Loucester, a worthy roast tube for offspring, he thinks: >My Lady, let me ask only one question to you, I beg to move the motion to hold your noble hand in mine. This amendment of our lives fulfils a commitment, and we gave on our valuable genes to our lucky descendants. Let us be our self start-up associated for each other. I carry the costs and you will assist me. It´s very difficult to become qualifying personal as soon as possible for these - ehem- special things. Comply and so on.< Even though her name sounded old, she was only a fresh twenty something. Certainly not ready to give in to this old fogey. But she would take the money, unabashedly. Finally was Sir Rob a Lord Beau-Mont of Wisthley, she was sensitive to names and gold and money: >I have only one question at this point, can you confirm that there is no terrible little catch somewhere behind all this? Can you noble Lord also confirm that you will possibly spend your money for your children?< Sir Rob noted the plural, they would have sex with each other at least twice. Good, good! This was an aim in his age. Lady Sophie thought of how she could foist her children on him. Not too rushed, step by step. >Then it´s nothing wrong, what I understand for this.< she said. >It´s shall, of course. What else can one man expect who is so lucky as me in this time?< Sir

Robs trial and error was successful in the end!

>You better neuter that mutt!< said her mother on Lady Sophies next call. In the dignified language of the old nobility. That also thought Bob when Sir Rob told him about the wedding. Where Sir Rob constantly used the word mating, not wedding. >How did it go?< Bob ask. >I know what you´re feeling.< Sir Rob answer: >The endless rat race in the dschungel of upper class and her no rational law in social conditions ends now. I´m now trapped in my little cage of love.< >Hold your horses.< said Bob. >I will show of the bride next time to you. It is as cabin fever is over for a long time now.< Sir Rob raved about his newly awakened love. Under pressure Bob works powerful and this was a very punchy situation, Bob will seen neither cloud nine nor honeymoon. He bit the bullet and will be unpleasant but necessary, he works now in Bulldozer mode on the worlds stage in business: >Straight fire for us both! Flexible your live and your Business, if I was in your shoes, I will do the same. When the last ball rolls you take what you can get.< Sir Rob looked puckish; >Pardon, my son?<

>Pardon?< the line manager asked Bob: >He will marriage a chick?< >Eh, language!< answered Bob. >Shut up. Me blow a fuse. What on earth is the whoremonger thinking?< >I believe ...< >Do you think really, your opinion interests me? Pull yourself together!< You could too, Bob thought. But he preferred to remain silent now. >Yet the fact that a girl can be found

55

on her majesty list doesn´t make it acceptable for us. The job for Sir Rob is to describe our hoover as a single crankier man with leave no stone unturned. This works only without a woman on his side.< Getting praise from Bob has bolstered his line manager confidence, so Bob said: >You´re right!< >Action speaks louder than words. Do something, quick.< said his boss.

Bob did something, he visited Baroness Sophie of Loucester and her disgusting little screamers. There could be no talk of an orderly conversation. Both children were really ugly, not housebroken and full of nasty words, when it rains it pours. It's the English upper class he's narked with and he knows it's time to leave behind his love affair with a certain kind of Englishness. This was exactly the point: no more false consideration, it was also about his money, work and job. Bob banged his fist on the table: >Finish now! It is not possible.< However in the end Bob was amazed at what was possible. Sophie was not only noble and a single mother. She was clever, greedy for titles and money. In this case a successful combination. For the YAM-group and Bob, too. Sir Rob would never get his longed for swap of bodily fluids, that was Bob already certain now. The bad-looking little grimace of the boy, possessed quite different abilities. He was a nerd. Not only looked like this. In under three minutes he cracked Sir Rob's account and change this or that. And the daughter was photogenic. Again, Bob making his calculation without Sir Rob.

It is always darkest before the dawn and with all the lollys Sir Rob fell back into old habits. A beer does no harm, a second neither. Here a whiskey, there a line. It´s always sunny in Sir Rob's Home. With the proper amount of alcohol and such other things in his body, he shot a new video clip. Now his time has come. He believe in good stories. And this internet thing was a damned good story, only for the wrong people. Sir Rob respect his followers in many ways, the most important was their money. However, they are only good for table tremble, he knows what he will in future: honour! From the old fancy bulls, he always wrangled with. Aristocracy does not sleep. He didn't believe in a defensive crouch. Sir Rob had have seen enough of those poor lives of former grand dukes without power and money where they stripped down for everything. Now he came. In reality these clips are a lack luster performance to date. Sir Rob was not quite sober, he could barely stand. In this ecstasy he thought it was a great idea to lie down in the bathtub with the hoover today. And the water was running in. Among from the things, he shouldn´t do under any circumstances, this was right at the top, he had signed something like this. The only reason Sir Rob got this idea with the water was because he had read it and always, they wanted to stop him having fun. That was a near one. But enemies of some form or other lurked on every side. Allegedly to his safety, but he wouldn't have it. Well, water and the Yam hoover, these were two things that got along very well. Now their finding their perfect match, they reacted to each other immediately. >Stuff happens< Sir Rob thought and nothing more after that.

Most people feel, from time to time, that their work is meaningless. For Bob this is to beat a dead horse. Less attention would be more for him. >At lowest the wedding is off the table. See at least. Call it a day and miss the boat.< said the line manager. >Not quite, not quite.< Bob answered. >He could deal with it, he´s death!< >Yes, above all yes. And no!< >Means?< asked the line manager stunned. >Perhaps we ask us the right questions. Baroness Sophie of Loucester was closed to Sir Rob. They had a pre-contract. She inherits everything< said Bob. > Where did you get this? You trust her?< >In this point yes.< >Could it in everything only be incremental improvements for us, are we riding always a burning pig: Off to a bright future. Riding two burning pigs?< >Three, she had two kids.< >Marvelous!< >Maybe Sophie is a bit smarter than she looks, how else could you explain making her to his wife in no time?< >His last gag?< >It´s so mad.< >Dear God it's all rather hard to take in!< >Only for Sophie, I think, she will treat herself next times.< >We wouldn´t burn bridges. Talk to her!< And Bob will visiting Sophie a second time.

>His one-liner was flat as a pancake. What we are all missing is the quirkiness, as well as the ambiguity, the bumpy irregularities that make clips so exasperating and so wonderful. When our wires get crossed and we have legs to understand one another, this is what we have been done. My kids and I. We continue this. Funnier, more demanding, better, could you try telling a knock-knock joke in Latin. It will be an extraordinarily rich broth

of happiness!< Sophie called Bob:> Bad jokes terms relish the most of us about as much as a vampire does garlic!< Sophie ends. And Bob was finished, too.

>Blessing in disguise< said Bobs line manager. He was quite enraptured by this idea. Bobs Boss only wondered why he hadn't thought of it: >Many people can't tell the difference between fun and funny. Sophie seems to be able to do it. Not bad at all.< And further he said: >Fix it! These are our people. Time will prove it. Publish it in the papers. It can´t wait.< When Bob was already standing in the hallway his boss brought him back: >Don´t give the party pooper! You are responsible to me for everything. Still!< Bob Only thought: >Get me out there!<

The mother of Lady Sophie looks full of pride of her daughter when they moved into the castle: >Sir Rob was head over heels about you. However, you bit the bullet! And you are a talented forger as well!< >You said: I better neuter that mutt!< >Yes, it never hurts!< >Done!< Both looked happy for their new life.

stay lead
Mikos Meininger 2017

Hardcore Salesman

Rupert Henckelmann isn´t only the Head of Sales of the Lip Care/Facial Care Business Unit (pronounced: Business Unit F.A.C.), but also he is THE sales professional at Jensen Kopp Ltd. His sales successes are already legendary. Every day a big story, a big win. Rupert has always been responsible for the sales training of the sales rookies. One week of tips and tricks from a high professional. Of course, one week is not enough to turn lambs into sales killers. But they are learning all about motivation. When life gives you lemons, order salt and a tequila. Rupert is full of these helpful sayings. Selling also consists of many frustrating experiences and Rupert cushions them perfectly.

How many of the trainees came to thank him! For recognising the first stumbling blocks, for praising the customer for his purchase after a deal and many more topics. At Jensen Kopp, everyone knows that if there is a sales professional, it´s Rupert.

Once a professional - always a professional. Also, on holiday.

Rupert does not avoid sales situations. No, he even seeks them out. When he can, he drives his family to markets, small boutiques and talks to every street vendor. This may be very annoying for the family, but for Rupert there is only one slogan: do it, do it, do it. Practice is everything! This summer, Rupert and his family are spending their quality time in Florence. Or in Italian: Firenze. No big deal. A flat on the wine route, a pool, nice curves for the company car, BeMmdouppelUuu , number 5; to be exact, a 535i with 3000 euros paying of its own and more than two hundred horsepower. Not too small, not too big. Just in keeping with his status quo.

There are various markets in Florence, and Rupert wants to experience them all. His wife, the reality-brake, still stands between his wishes and her reality. He is not allowed to experience his first market until Thursday. Disappointingly, Florence City is very small, the are running very quickly through the market. Every stall offers leather bags. Rupert is particularly taken with one, an "I Medici" or so, he didn´t understand the real name. Two separate pockets inside, one for a laptop. A smaller further one for business cards and two pens is sewn into the back. Two extra pockets are sewn onto the front, one just big enough for his mobile. There are two flaps on top. He has no idea what they are for, but the flaps don't bother him. The bag is available in black, red, dark brown and light brown or multicolored. For him as a big fish, of course, comes only the serious and yet casual-looking dark brown bag into consideration. Only: it doesn't stand on its own! Falls in every case and lies flat on the ground. But: Is not every perfect beauty, blessed with the flaw of an imperfection?

As a hard seller, he has his pride. No matter how beautiful the bag is, no one is going to take him for a ride. He takes his time. A good deal takes time or is very fast. Time can´t run out in this case. He turns and turns the bag, pulls each zip open twice and closed three times.

Meanwhile, the salesman tells Rupert about the advantages of his bag. Rupert, of course, pretends not to listen. Nevertheless, he thinks the quality described is good. He sees the neatly finished seams, hears that this piece of jewellery is made in Italy, not in China. Rupert sees the difference in quality clearly. The greed increases, this bag should be it. In the small compartment is the note with the price. Rupert opens and closes all the zips again and, purely by chance, also takes a look at the note: 356 euros. Dream on, (keep dreaming) poor devil, thinks Rupert.

>Quanta costa?< asks Rupert.

>Treeheeehundretfifty, but for you tuhundrettwenty!< the salesman smiles at him. A tooth is missing. It's not about beauty, it's about business, he admonishes himself.

Rupert shakes his head. >Tuu muuusch. Iss tuu muuusch.<

>What iss your laaastpreeice?< the entire upper tooth front minus one points at Rupert.

This is the peak of the sales curve, now or not, this is where the salesman's adrenaline is at its highest. Inwardly, Rupert laughs. What he has a huge advantage. He not only knows the theory, he is also a practitioner. A hard seller. Somehow Rupert has remained a human being, he feels sorry for the salesman, the poor guy can't help his lack of training. Yes, here would be waiting a lot of work for Rupert Henckelmann.

>Onhundretfifty< says Rupert, what counts yet is speed. Numbers are better numbers, if they are coming fast now. First put down the opponent slowly, then defeat him by surprise. It could be Sun Tsu, Konfuzius or Lao Tse. Or an other big asian leader, it´s not important right now.

The salesman whistles, turns around and calls: >Mario, centocinquanta?<

>No< it calls out from behind the stall.

The salesman smiles, takes the bag in his hand and put it away.

Rupert doesn´t give up, he dosn´t stop so easily: >Whhhat is yuur last preeice?<

>Oonhundredeteeeihty<

Rupert rejoices and chimes in. He saved a lot of money. Someone should try to copy him.

His wife asks him: >Are you crazy? There are only fantasy prices on the market and the bag would certainly be cheaper. On this market, in this street or in the whole town!< Here Rupert again notices the difference between the educated layman, his wife, and him, the professional. His wife is often right about small things, but that's because he doesn't care whether the mustard costs 1.20 or 1 Euro 65. His slogan is: Save on the big things, then you have more for the small.

The amateur doesn't see the big picture, nor can she. Although he is always a little disappointed in his wife, ten years ago he chose her according for intellectual criteria. Really a pity, this.

He sees the end of the holidays, one day before, he can hardly wait for his grand entrance with the new bag. His secretary Rosy is a bag fan. Oh, a bag groupie. He packs his laptop, his business cards, two pens, one writing in red (!), and his mobile into the "I Medici". He now only calls the bag the "I Medici". Rupert thinks this makes the bag look even more expensive. Of course, it falls over first. It's their own fault, Rupert thinks to himself - if you don't pack properly! Think a little, if you are packing your things. Only when he turns the laptop and puts it in the middle compartment and puts the business cards in the back, does the bag stands on its own. The jewel! Perfect.

On Monday morning Rosy is already sitting at her desk, unfortunately Liselotte Hunniger is standing with her. The secretary of the marketing line manager, some say, she has only got her job because ... well, rumours.

He greets them both and holds the "I Medici" in his hand. So that both women have to see it. Rosy has another question, gets the signature folder and asks him to sign something quickly.

This is the big option: Rupert puts the bag on the table. The "I Medici" falls flat to the front and lies there awkwardly. Between the coffee cup and the computer keyboard.

>I bought a bag like that from Florence. You can buy it at any market for no more than 50 euros. Nice<, says Liselotte Hunniger and leaves the office. >Mine is red<, says his secretary.

stay nice
Mikos Meininger 2017

Once upon a time there was a managing director who discovered: Firing is no fun at all! And so, middle management came along to the company and the world of management. The other managers saw this and liked it. And of course, they copied him. At some point, a university professor discovered his market niche and invented the important sandwich layer, i.e. the middle of the sandwich.

From then on, it was good form for a company to have a middle layer. This cemented itself, formed a wall. Older and more mature, it then became the clay layer or paralysis layer. Everything stands still if they put anything out of action. Young, fresh companies formed it out of glass as soon as enough money was available. Only one thing was always the same about this layer: it was and is impenetrable. For women, for experts and every human that is not of white ethnicity. Two wonderful concepts created new jobs, or vice versa.

So that no one noticed how unpleasant this position was, there was training. Training on finding teams, on motivation, on hiring processes, on staff development. The nice thing about the training for the providers was that every few years the people in middle management were completely replaced. This meant that the training could start all over again. Only there was never any training for dismissals.

Middle management always worked those out for themselves,

through hard social pain. Loneliness, broken marriages, and the long evenings at the hotel bar. Then, when they were finally ready, the company had to go lean. And a lean sandwich still has bread on the top and bottom, just less coleslaw in the middle. In such an externally celebrated turnaround, middle management went home alone every three to six years. They left voluntarily, under pressure or simply for operational reasons.

Of course, the middle of the company was always too thick, too many people, with tasks that were too unclear. That's why companies sought external advice. Often at the end of a wave of layoffs. And at the beginning. The external consultants then liked to say: You have to become leaner! You are still far too fat! Too many unproductive people are sitting in your midst. Only when the two halves of the sandwich touched each other, and the top management was threatened with disgusting work did the call go out to the management: "more middle management is a MUST!" Bread on bread, that doesn't taste good for general managers. The previously expensively advised gaps were closed again, the onerous work was pushed into the new middle, the youth were given a chance. Quarterly, half-yearly or even annually, it came down to everyone. The motivational staff development meeting! Surely the centre managers should do that.

Now murder is not always the first thought at an appraisal interview. Not in the case of the manager who is dealing with an employee's shortcomings. And often not for the employee either, who may not particularly like this ritual, but endures it. After all, appraisal interviews mean: Give healthy feedback on the respective performance status! Motivating words at the beginning and at the end, execution in between. Murder is then often only the second thought. Often arises with the second sentence of the evaluator and begins with: >You ...<

There are damn few murdered bosses. Why is that? The magic formula of the praised level is: middle management! The obstacle for the ordinary employee to kill someone is responsibility. Who is the target, who do I owe all this nonsense to? My boss, the boss above, the company policy, my union representative who supports me politically and nothing else. Or management, maybe a shareholder?

Like a school of fish, responsibility flows past the person being judged. It is difficult to concentrate on a culprit, let alone find one. The whole thing is a multi-causal failure, so to say! Organized irresponsibility, as authorities can't do any better.

>Are you even listening to me anymore?< the boss shouted, staring at Mikel. Mikel him now too: >Oh, I´m ... no longer make sense in the portfolio.< Mikel quickly repeated the last words said. Twenty years of marriage were not for nothing! Still, those six words made no sense. Mikel swallowed. Anything from downsizing to product elimination was possible now. His boss squinted his left eye briefly, shrugged his shoulder and continued to glare

to himself. With the slide deck of his PowerPoint presentation, created by the People Organization Department, in short known as PO. Simply Human Resources was no longer enough.

Mikel´s boss did not fully know her himself yet. Only the junior PO assistant. She had drafted the presentation in a nutshell three weeks ago, quickly, as an additional project. Then sent it to middle management for correction, got no response, found it good, passed it on. Now this presentation was the basis of the staff meeting. Michael's boss went through his workload, and heavily laid the tasks on him. Checking thought experiments of the PO department, there was no time for that. Someone would have already checked the presentation, after all, it had been released. What else was he supposed to do? All he had left to do was a stand-up presentation. He was a master at that, he thought. Unfortunately, only he was.

Mikel had long seen through his superior. Competence was not one of his strengths. Feedback meetings only took place at Mikel´s level; his boss was, after all, upper middle management! He was about to jump the career ladder. He chaired this year's feedback culture debate. It had come about like this: The PO department reminded the management about the upcoming staff appraisals. Already the cascade began quickly and effectively, always with a hint of reproach in the voice: >Have you already ...?< Of course, nobody had prepared anything. So it finally hit the youngest: >Make it.< And she did, producing eighty-two slides for a two-hour talk. 82 (!) slides of jumble. A mix of values from the homepage, values from the speeches of the managing director and his faithful, ideas that were still following from university, and all copied and fixed. String copy; a >best of< full of thoughts, inspirations and flashes of inspiration. Much of it had also been copied from the homepage of a competitor.

In his own company, no one had cared about values for years. No time for this stuff. That's why no one watched this presentation any more. For a variety of reasons: Reasons! The next two weeks simply passed too quickly. And so there were eighty-two unfiltered slides lying around.

The PO department distributed them by email. After the mails, another handout reached middle management by post. Better safe than sorry. Finally, the slides went out to the entire staff. Mikel was one of the first to get it.

His boss, too, of course. There was no time for preparation. Mikel´s boss didn't waste any time on preparation anyway. They both knew that. Mikel was presented with unfiltered strong stuff.

>Questions?< barked Mikel´s boss; with the clear message: >Don´t be sad? < It went on. The monotone voice, lacking any timbre, echoed through the room. Raised neither interest, nor brought any insight or other annoying gain. Mikel nodded unnoticed for a moment. Suddenly there was silence. Mikel wrenched his eyes open, startled. However, his boss was struggling with the technology.

Lurking in slide sixty-two was a gimmick from the junior PO assistant, a hidden Excel file. In the middle of the slide they both saw a large red dot. The mouse pointer demanded to be clicked. Mikel´s boss clicked and clicked. First left, then right, then both. Nothing happened. The junior PO assistant's computer skills did not intersect with those of Mikel´s boss or middle management. They did not even touch. The programme should have been opened before, so it just produced one system crash after another. One curse followed the next, until in the end it was: >Where is that chick?< If sexual equality doesn´t exist in your mind, in a stressful situation your true colours come out.

Furious, Mikel´s boss ran out of the office, all he heard was: > ... immediately ... straight away ... now ... this rubbish ... no function ... not with me ...< the door swallowed the rest. Mikel looked at the slides. In the background he read as a title: Two E's for us and our customers: Efficiency and Effectiveness! Mikel suddenly sat wide awake at the table. Wasn't the company's motto: We want to get a little better every day!!!? He leafed through his notepad. There it was in black and white, the motto: Take a small step forward every day, for the very big leap forward! He googled the two E's; efficiency and effectiveness. Found them on the most important competitor; probably not only him.

Silence, smirk. Now that was stupid. His mood was mixed between the elation of a discovered mistake and the depressing truth: our company is now already writing off the competitor.

There was a loud noise outside, then someone shouted: >Help!< Slowly he rose. Was this a trap or real? It was real! In the corridor lay his boss, next to him stood the junior PO assistant and the executive assistant. While his boss was lying in front of them like that, clutching his chest, a colleague who had joined him asked: >Is your meeting over now? Are you through? Is the room free?< Mikel looked at him. Perplexed.

>No answer is an answer< said the colleague. More people came and went. One said: >Not my department.< And left again. No one helped, no one called an ambulance. >What an underperformer!< it flashed through Mikel´s mind. In his mind still completely in the evaluation system of the appraisal interview.

>That's the problem with middle management, just like with a heart attack. Both are useless< thought the executive assistant. And if they haven't died, then they are still alive today ....

stay there
Mikos Meininger 2017

Every ascent brings work with it. Brings the unexpected to light. Emma Al-Jedi looked at her emails: Seven hundred! From last night to this morning. Seven hundred! Working in an international company was all well and good, albeit a 24/7 job. But this was tantamount to a job creation scheme. Next to the German colleagues came the emails from the Americans and then the emails from Asia. India at the end. While the Indians dipped every word in a different colour and some of the emails were impossible to read or in Hindi, Emma wondered about the aggressive tone of the Americans and the lack of salutation of the Germans. A new broom sweeps clean. Emma will sweep.

She immediately sat down to write an email etiquette book. First she formulated the deadly sins: writing everything in CAPITAL LETTERS, sin number one. Then sarcasm. The repetitive replies with the title line: Re:- Re:- Re:- Re:- Re:- Re:- Re:- Re:- Re:- which were just forwarded and where Emma had to scroll to the end to even get close to knowing what it might be about. Then there were the cowardly emails that shifted responsibility, where the author was too cowardly to simply make a phone call. Or the cowardly ones without a sender or the blind copies. That is a big no-no. Or do you see a dog poo as a gift?

However, Emma found the daring emails the worst. The ones without meaning. They constantly asked what it meant, whether it could be. Each time with a very unsatisfactory answer. E-mails that wasted time, hampered decisions and produced nothing but electrical waste. Emma wrote: unclearly written emails are time wasters! They are to be refrained from. Ok, now that wasn't worded in a friendly way either. She would revise the whole thing later.

Then Emma devoted an entire paragraph to the subject line. Empty did not work at all. It should always contain the reason for the email, at least. She formulated the rule: A glance reveals your request, the place and the time. There is only one reason to use blind copy, but which one was it. Emma leafed through the Standard Operating Process/ SOP. Yes, there is: protect the recipient's privacy, in the case of a large mailing list, even outside the company. She adopted the wording. Good things for good writing are always right, or better: not wrong.

Emma tried to formulate her discomfort, why did so much go wrong in the email traffic? Because it's so easy to send an email. That was it! She formulated the next rule: after reading, at least two hours must pass before you write a reply. Correct.
The next point Emma herself found tricky was the greeting. E-mails tended to become looser in the course of correspondence. The >Dear Sirs or Dear Sir and Madam ...< changed with each reply into shorter and shorter words, and in the end are omitted altogether. E-mails are levellers, they suggest closeness where there is none. Formal remains standard! Another point dealt with.

Emma was making progress; it wasn't even nine o'clock yet.

Humans love themselves the most, so they always think their issues have priority. They like to raise the red flag, whether the mail is important or not. Southern European men liked to press the flag symbol. Emma thought: Is this a replacement for the car horn or are they so unsure of themselves that they have to make everything important? She didn't know, but saw the point. No flag, without a reason or a need!

Then the copy line. Who comes in, when in the copy. Emma chose the easy way: who is concerned, works on the project or gives budget for it. Everyone else is to be avoided. That was easy.

Now for the read receipt. Emma found it intrusive. Not just an email, but a follow-up email and preferably a confirmation email. If the issue was so important, why not call instead? She worded it as friendly as possible for her in this morning situation.

Her email account lit up. A new email from her secretary. She was blatantly making fun of Emma, had edited a video together and underlaid it with disgusting comments. That was good. Emma hadn't thought of that at all: emails sent by mistake. She formulated it like this, first write the emotions, then think about it for a moment, then create the subject line and think about it again. Read over it again and then edit the >To< line.

She went through the whole text, checked the spelling and sent the rules to everyone. She forwarded the video from her secretary to the personnel manager. >Dear Hannes, you can surely see for yourself that the relationship of trust is broken. Please transfer or dismiss my secretary, I don't care. I don't want to see her in my office again this afternoon. Love, Emma<

The next mail went to her friend: >Dear Carolin, it's done. This afternoon you can move into your new workplace in my anteroom. I am looking forward to it and am surprised myself by the speed. We will rock this company together! Emma.<

Two minutes later Hannes answered. That was quick. Unfortunately, he used the >Re:< function. It was the email to Carolin! >Dear Emma, I think we have something to discuss. Please come to my office around 11 o'clock. Hannes< Emma felt bad. She would revise the paragraph with the accidentally sent emails, if she was still there at that point.

stay calm
Mikos Meininger 2017

Gemma

>And, now? Are you´re here or is it only your body?<

Gemma looks at me. I sit in front of the signature folder full of expectation. A pen in my hand. Ready to go to extremes, ready to sign. Sign some documents. I´m the line manager, for first time in my life.

>Aren't you going to open the folder?<

Four people sit in the room: three secretaries and me. And three pairs of eyes fix their gaze on me. Gemma moves her office chair backwards. Four centimeters of space, it seems longer and deeper than the Grand Canyon.

Friendly Gemma smiles at me: >And everything else is okay with you?<

Gemma is my secretary. In the hierarchy pyramid, as well as in the organization chart, clearly below my position, below me. On the other hand, she organizes my appointments, my events and much more, some of which I am not even aware of. And don't want to know. Knowledge is a burden. Not knowing is the liberty of a good boss. Decisions are very easy, if you don't know what they are about.

My motto since university has been as far as her knowledge about my job is concerned, she is clearly above me.

The charged atmosphere in the room does not go unnoticed by me. As a communication expert, this is more of a test than a danger. In a matter of seconds, I briefly go through all the communication models I know, to see which one fits. The advantage of these models is that they are all theoretical! And at the moment - .... none of them really fit.

Three pairs of eyes are still focused on me and my pen, which I am holding in the ready position. As a behavioral trainer, I know that animals react with flight or attack. I try attack. I look Secretary III deeply and sharply in the eye. Then Secretary II says: >We should demand an aggravation premium. After all, we work with executives who are difficult to educate and untrainable.<

Aha! Stage II. Escalation, it immediately goes into my head. Should I briefly explain the 4-Ears Model or answer with APO? Or was it ADO? Another model comes to my mind, funnily enough not the name, except that it was first mentioned by Goethe. While I'm thinking about it, I've missed Secretary II's next line. Besides, I'm still working on secretary III. I feel like I've been sitting there for a quarter of an hour with my pen in my hand. To sharpen my sense of the time that has passed, I glance at my watch.

When I look around again, I realize my mistake. Now the

air is really on fire and is thicker as London fog in October. Only more fiery, not so wet. Alone I´m wet.

How about escape? The way to the door, an estimated four meters. I would have to put the chair back, take my coat, my bag and quickly leave the room. Oh yes! And the signature folder. Add a snappy remark and the situation would be cleared up. Nothing than as a black eye in my mind.

If it weren't for Secretary II. >I guess someone has management border-line!< Satisfied, the three of them look at me. They laugh inside themselves.

Then my boss comes in. >And why are you so cheerful here?<

>Friedrich has a severe nervous condition. He can't open the signature folder< says Gemma.

My boss smiles. Whenever he doubts, he smiles. How much stronger his smile is, the situation was more inevitable, tricky isn´t? >And Friedrich, what do you say to that?

Now models really don't help any more, we need something with substance. A base, or something with foundation. Generally valid but profound, meaningful without significance, a guideline without orientation. But what? Suddenly an idea twitches through my mind. Last week at the seminar, what was it at the end? Yes, exactly: >You have to accept feedback all the time!< I say.

My boss laughs. Everyone in the room laughs.

I take the signature folder, make my three signatures, take my things, and go outside with my boss. I would call it an elegant escape; I have no idea what I signed.

>You are an ace-communicator < he says appreciatively.

>Yes, I think they really like me.< I reply.

stay cool
Mikos Meininger 2017

Naples

Gomorrah. One word describes Naples as it is, as it lives, has always lived. Who would want to go on holiday there? I never did. My girlfriend was born there. She wanted to. Back home. So did her friends. Italy, the land where the lemons bloomed. We didn't waste any thought on plans, managing business or budgets. Just living, in the here and now. >Better to feel the breath of death every day?< But my objection was laughed away. Sun, summer - here we come. A car without scratches? >We are going to Italy! Think about it. We're not going to take my new car.< Holger said while still in Germany. Ricarda's old Fiat station wagon carried us over the Alps.

The rented flat was in *Via Atri*, in the middle of the old town. It was the extension of *Via Nilo*, which led to the hills of *Caponapoli*. Greeks built their acropolis there and there was a temple for the siren Parthenope on top. Naples the Strange, much lived only in memory or from it. Reality was often out of reach. Longing was something of a permanent state of mind here. Mine sank when I saw the street.

For tourists like us, the narrow *Via Atri* was without attraction. It stood almost empty in space. Remains of city walls crumbled nothing. Next to wrecked cars, heaps of rubbish and fluttering laundry, the baroque façade of our house was crumbling. At night it was dim. Dark. To the right and left were palazzi with spectacular architectural courtyards, often destroyed, the staircases wandering through time as ghostly ruins. Summer smelled of old fish, cat urine and exhaust fumes from various mopeds. Of course, there was also rubbish. Neighbours reported that in winter the smell of burnt wood from the ovens of the Sorbillo pizzeria and frying fat from the backyard kitchens added to the smell.

The road has run here for two and a half thousand years; - Vergil walked along it, as did Goethe. And now, us. Holger with Ricarda at the front, then Mariella and me. Goethe described the cheerful evenings with his friend Gaetano Filangieri; - his family inhabited the entire second floor of the Palazzo Belvedere. The only thing cheerful today was the view over the Gulf of Naples, which fascinated Goethe. The view seemed indestructible. In contrast to the flat. Almost unbelievable in this city. The ceiling frescoes under which Goethe dined still hung in the Belvedere, but now an amiable Neapolitan lawyer lived there. The next week he proudly showed Holger his collection of Mussolini and Hitler memorabilia. I had not expected that. Mariella said this was not her Naples. A lot had changed. Ricarda just laughed.

We only walked a few steps to the corner of *Via dei Tribunali* and *Via Nilo*. Here a taxi dropped us off once in the evening, the driver said worriedly: >There is no hotel here.< >And no penhouse suite< he added quickly. Mariella, my love, answered him in Italian, the reply in his language reassured him a little. Ricarda laughed her bright, infectious laugh again. The Campari sat deep with me, the hormones sat high and ready for everything. For the first time, I looked at Ricarda rather than Mariella. Still, I had no idea about Naples or the south of Italy until now. Foolhardy and completely unreasonable, the journey still seems to me today, even decades later. This question kept coming up: >Why Naples of all places?< Even the landlord of the holiday flat was surprised. After two days, Holger and Mariella walked hand in hand. It smelled like separation - without pain. I only saw Ricarda. Mariella said Naples wasn't her thing anymore. Her parents were spending the summer at the beach in Rome. They would follow them, Holger and her.

The landlord was pleased that Ricarda and I stayed longer. In Palazzo Spinelli, the ceiling had collapsed shortly before. More precisely, the historic wooden ceiling, the ceiling of our living room. Newly in love, we slept, ate and lived in the small guest room for the first while. The rest of the flat was occupied by quickly erected scaffolding, which only provisionally supported the remaining ceiling beams. Of course, the windows were not tight. *Tarpaulins* stretched next to the mountains of rubble, rattling in the icy wind at night. The wind spoke to us through the leaky window cracks. We only slept more deeply.

I heard: >Go, go home!< Ricarda heard: >Home, this is where I want to live.< In the morning we sat on the terrace, each sipping our *café correto*. The two peaks of *Vesuvius* nestled in the light blue sky and Ricarda said: >Here it's very different from

Trentino, where I grew up. This is Italy. Do we want to stay here? < Inwardly, of course, I didn't say anything, but love came out of my mouth: >Whatever you want!< I looked at us sitting there, saw our mutual deep affection and thought: Oh, what the hell. And no matter how pretty such a volcano was, my plan was not to go that deep into this juggernaut. Without getting too far ahead of myself, all I can say is, first this happens, and then that happens, it's much later that somehow too much happens. And everything that happens, happens in these years.

We spent the rest of the week looking for a flat. Through Mariella's parents, it happened very quickly. Much too quickly. Confused by the charm of the old Neapolitan buildings, we made a big mistake. We rented a large, cheap flat, which then couldn't be heated in winter. It was on the noisiest street in town, and we renovated it at our own expense with meticulous German precision. Our bourgeois neighbors called us *un po' folle*, which was just meant in jest, but even the youngest son told us: a real Neapolitan would never have done that. We were also duped by the dialect. Neapolitan was completely incomprehensible even to Ricarda.

The first months in Naples were hard: the greengrocer in the *Sanità* market, a robust neighbourhood, cheated us every day. Politely, we ate the greasiest dishes in bad trattorias and waited for hours for trains on the *Metropolitana*. In the mornings I learned Italian, Ricarda worked. In our big flat we rented out three rooms for backpackers. What we got didn't even recoup part of the renovation costs. And our guests complained about lack of sleep. The thin windows filtered neither smells nor the traffic of the night. *Via Santa Teresa degli Scalzi* was alive twenty-four hours a day! Here the cars and trucks rushed to the airport and to the *tangenziale*, the city motorway.

While I was guiding additional strangers, Ricarda opened a shop: Dresses, swimwear, underwear. Of course, it went wrong. One trial followed the next. We won them all. Even in the last instance, but the Italian justice system only made *Kafka* proud. Legally binding sentences disappeared into the abysses of an astonishingly inefficient southern Italian judicial system, the sentences were not enforced for years, and we ran out of breath. My hair turned grey.

That evening, the fireworks exploded in the sky more than usual. They were not celebrations in the sense of joy, they were the news channels of the *Camorra* clans who kept each other informed in the old quarter through the *fuochi artificiali*. Not even the rat family in the courtyard was disturbed. In our huge kitchen we only heard the Garibaldi sisters, their daily quarrels were always about death, often about money and only sometimes about men. They lived on the first floor, we on the third: >I have to die!< >Then hurry up!<

Almost every Sunday, they invited us into their living room, drank their watery tea, ate their dry biscuits and learned everything about our neighbors. Even those we didn't know at all. Just before we left, the inevitable question came: >When will it be?< In this city, nothing is impossible, why not conceive a child? But before that, I destroyed every neighbourly relationship with a boiled litre of water. The sons in the fourth were nocturnal, all possessed engines of every kind without exhaust or silencer. The last roar of the engine was followed by a squeak of the gate, a whistle of the children and noisy gestures of farewell. Loudly. Then the footsteps rumbled up the stairs and the door fell into the lock with a loud thud. That evening, while still in a sleep-like trance, I boiled a litre of water and tipped it into the yard. Wild shouting followed. Then silence. Until we moved out, no one in the house spoke to us again.

But all these adversities did not take away the boldness, we knew Naples, then *Campania* and the whole south. An unknown country in the middle of Europe. A single great mystery, the noise during the day faded gently in the evening, the streets sank back into their ancient millennia of history. This ancient Greco-Roman city that *Curzio Malaparte* called: Naples, as Pompeii never buried, this magical projection of our desires remained exciting. It was our nightly walks *through Via Anticaglia* or *Piazza San Gaetano* in which we fell even more in love, with ourselves, with Naples. We also saw a flat, unique in *Via San Biagio dei Librai*. Again, a palazzo. On one balcony we grew vegetables, on the terrace we lived on the third we slept. On hot summer nights the *Libeccio* came from Africa, carrying the sand from the Sahara with it, then we woke up as if powdered. The seagulls screamed, the chaos was natural, the neighbourhood familiar. We lived like we were in a village.

We lived in Naples in spite of everything. The neighbors mingled, their were bizarre personalities. University professors, like petty criminals, craftsmen, bourgeois, and families completely the opposite. Old nobility and the most garish lower-class proletariat, all human possibilities of existence lived here. That remained the charm of Naples, a city where no one need starve or be lonely. There were neighbors I had never seen fully dressed. And then there was Monique.

The mistress of a small Camorra boss in the neighborhood. There was an aura about her, wicked, full of grandeur. Monique called me Professore because of my glasses. She always wanted something from me. Be it her supposed birthday or a name day, a donation was always required., at every chance encounter. Otherwise, the tires were broken, the bicycle destroyed or there was a fire in the hallway. The worst was the annual procession of the *Virgin Maria*. At first glance, people were running behind a silver-plated statue of the *Virgin Maria*, stopping just outside Monique's door. It could have been a breather for the porters, maybe the procession wanted to wait for those behind. No, this was not about praising a Mother of God, here they were paying homage to Monique. She was about to ascend; the neighborhood was becoming hers. That's why the inhabitants bowed to her, *inchino* they called it. The criminals' calculation remained simple, if even a statue of *Maria* bowed to them, then they were truly worthy of being worshipped. Monique became the object of the cult. Especially in southern Italy, the priest is often very close to the mafia. For the Church here was always the shepherd for all God's children. It was the blessing for the Mafia, for Monique.

Her body was the instrument of her political power. Her voice, her energy, her laughter. We heard it everywhere in the neighborhood. Pregnant women asked her to put her hand on their belly. Her body was her brand, it said I made it because I am beautiful, because I am sly and because I am better than all of you put together. After a bout of flu, she came back more energized and gave her business another boost. No virus crippled her, no heart condition or cancer. She was victorious. Always.

Memories are deceptive. Perhaps not everything was luck. Crises disappeared unnoticed, what remained was doubt. Temperament and only every conceivable Naples cliché lived in this house. Signora *Guida* drank *Limoncello*, sucked, smoked, mopped, and made phone calls. All at the same time. Her husband was constantly repairing the furniture she had destroyed. *Guida* stood at the market, since then we paid the right prices. We felt at home and the city changed from an open-air museum to a lively city inhabited by us. For the first time we really felt welcome. It was no longer a theatrical city, we were part of the theatre. Stubbornness, temperament, curiosity and generosity were no longer charms, it became our lifeblood. We were now as childishly self-indulgent as anyone in Naples. Ricarda got pregnant, that changed something. Everything.

Monique posted a video of her partying at the boss's mansion. The video showed a society that believed problems were only other people's conditions. A bunch of old men looked at naked girls dancing in front of them, undressing. The men were politicians, judges, respectable people in Naples. Drugs were on display. That evening they executed Monique in the street. That was the end of our one-sided love story with a city.

We sold our flat, gave up everything, on the way to the airport we drove past Via Atri, Palazzo Marigliano had become a tangle of B&B, hotels, and penthounses. >This is the hotspot of Airbnb apartments< said the young taxi driver. This is where it all began for us. >Maybe we should invest here?< I asked. But the Italian woman from *Trentino* was pregnant and had enough of the south. We moved to Germany. Gomorrah was behind us. We didn't turn around.

stay back
Mikos Meininger 2017

>Did you read instruction 39?<

>The 39? Yes, yes - terrible, isn't it?< replies Dr Schneider.

>Yes, terrible!< says Schnabel. He thinks about it and is silent.

Dr Schneider interrupts him: >How much time do we have left?<

>Six months until it officially goes to the press. Realistically three to four internally< Schnabel replies.

>You know, Mr Schnabel, my time budget is tight. I start with the first three lines and then decide according to importance. Have you read 39 to the end?< Dr Schneider looks at Schnabel questioningly.

Carsten Schnabel knows his superior only too well. But the fact that Dr Schneider did not even read papers with the highest urgency level now surprised him. He continued: >The 39 is based on the board decision of August last year ...<

>No basics, no phrases, Schnabel. Just the facts No fluff!< Dr Schneider urged. Only one hour until the business leaders' meeting, where he meets his colleagues. There is no time for Schnabel's endless explanations. So that Schnabel doesn't forget, he adds at the end: > ... and solutions!<.

Carsten Schnabel switches to the subordinate code, bends his back slightly forward and recites instruction 39. Flawlessly.

In the short time, however, especially the headings. It ends: >... which means we have to cut one third of the office staff by the end of the year. Announcement of the reduction: September!<

Dr Schneider lowers his eyes, chews on his pen, finally he says: >What a pity, isn´t it?< Inside him, the predator wakes up, takes a deep breath and asks: >How will the other business units react?<

Now it's Schnabel's time. Since Friday, he has been guile-lessly constantly phoning colleagues, emailing, and huddling in the tea kitchens of the different floors. Carsten Schnabel's network is glowing overall.

He knew everything, every rumor, every embarrassment, and suspected every action of the internal opponents in advance: >Nobody knows! Purchasing and warehouse are headless, both business managers were still enjoying their holidays last week, both had to cut their holidays short, they'll be at the meeting later. Only women work in the event service, two are pregnant. They are safe. The sales department will use the internal upheaval to strengthen its power. But there is a rumor ...< he swallows visibly, building tension, > ... about an affair; business head sales with secretary. That may not break a neck, but it can crack it!< Carsten Schnabel looks proudly at his boss.

Dr Schneider perceives his employee in a completely new way and then looks at the wall. Of course, the head of sales has a relationship with his secretary. After all, the four of them spend the weekend in a hotel - with their secretaries! How else could they have taken this course at company expense and told their wives? Schnabel, the idiot.

>Private life is taboo! Did you understand that Schnabel? T dot A dot B dot O dot O dot! I don't make a name for myself over the weaknesses of my colleagues. Where are your solutions? What do I have for the meeting?< Dr. Schneider yells at Schnabel, who is writhing in surprise. Irritated, he looks at his boss: >I thought ...<

>You thought? Thank you so much. Enough thinking, Schnabel, we still have half an hour. Have you prepared anything else?< Dr Schneider asks.

Carsten Schnabel hesitated: >I have thought about where the obstacles - ..., er stumbling, ..., no, where the step stones are. And how we get around them.<

>Now we're going in the right direction. Let's go then!< nods Dr. Schneider.

>Our company motto: Trust everyone - every day! doesn't really harmonize with restructuring. I see an insurmountable contradiction if the managers are to gain trust but then dismiss the employees. That doesn't fit.<

Dr Schneider eagerly takes notes. Carsten Schnabel continues: >That's why I imagine a new job, someone from outside who restructures. A game changer. This way we maintain the credibility of our internal colleagues, promote an external career and create a position that disposes of itself at the end of the year! < Schnabel is silent. >We are save and the patsy an outsider. Scapegoat goes out well done!< mumbles his boss to himself.

>Brilliant!< escapes Dr Schneider. >You are a genius, Schnabel. I won't forget this!< Dr Schneider stands up, puts on his jacket and accompanies Carsten Schnabel to the door. In the anteroom sits his secretary, a young, wonderfully pretty girl. He turns to Schnabel: >Great - thank you!< The employee Schnabel winks at the new pretty secretary as he walks. An unprecedented elation surge within him. Never before has his boss, Dr Schneider, thanked him. Never! And the new girl seems to fancy him, from the way she looked at the door. Wow, Instruction 39 accelerates his happiness.

Sure, of this, he prances down the corridor to his office. Who knows where this restructuring will take him!

Dr Schneider goes to the table: >And what do you think of him?< >Green, beige, brown – unobtrusive, pale, without colour. The perfect mister nobody, a typical Peter-Jim-and-Mary-Jane or better Jon Smith guy.< she looks at him. Sexual greed glows in the meeting point of their gazes. Dr Schneider interrupts the gaze, takes his transcript, and goes to the meeting. Determination and assertiveness signal his steps. Clack, clack, clack. He turns the corner and runs into the circle of his colleagues standing there.

>You're the last one, come on everybody inside, we're starting now!< says the line-manager. When everyone is seated, after the brief and informal greeting and a little joke, the managing director asks :>Has everyone read instruction 39? What do you think of it?<

A murmur fills the room, no one dares to make the first advance. Almost everyone present has only read 39 this morning or had it explained to them by their speaker.

>Bad, bad.< says the Head of Sales.

>And that's just when we're going through the trust-building process!< comes from the Head of Marketing.

The colleague from event management looks around: >Oh, you haven't finished with that yet? I have with my unit!<

>Are these your solutions?< asks the managing director. >I expected a bit more!<

Dr Schneider smells opportunity. He raises his hand, half-high. The managing director nods at him. >My solution looks at all the issues! A new position, filled with an external person. When the restructuring is over, the position becomes superfluous. We don't lose any trust, the external person gains experience. A clean solution. For us all.< Dr. Schneider looks triumphantly into the round.

>And how do you want to finance the position?< asks the managing director. Dr Schneider makes a sad face: >I would sacrifice my personal referee for it. Schnabel is a good one. But I have to think of the company, there is no room for selfishness!<

The managing director looks at Dr Schneider: >I wouldn't have thought that of you. I always thought you were such a softy. Not bad Schneider, not bad!< he looks around again.

>I would have expected something like that from any of you! Oh, and Schneider, send the beak to me in the personnel department later. I'll prepare everything. You have e-mail and mobile phone blocked now.< The managing director stands up: >Thank you, I think we have developed a good way today.<

On the way to his office, Dr Schneider is glowing. The managing director has never thanked him before! He enjoys this moment of respect; the office can wait - he goes to the tea kitchen. He drinks the espresso very slowly. His secretary hangs up the phone just as he enters the anteroom. >You are to come to the personnel department about this new appointment. You know why?> She looks at him questioningly. >All right, I'm on my way.< Dr Schneider walks the two floors, he feels so young and fit.

>And you really want to dismiss both of them?< the personnel manager asks the line-manager.

>How else are you going to finance the new position in restructuring management? We save two jobs, half a salary and gain a specialist!< says the managing director. >Wasn't it his own suggestion, I think so!<

stay clean
Mikos Meininger 2017

If the goal isn´t clear, nothing matters. More precisely, not everyone always has to know the goal. Why? It would be ideal; it is even better if one's own goal and the collective goal are known. For everyone. Anywise. Even for those it concerns. Let´s put it this way: if the boss doesn't know the goal, how is the rest of the company supposed to know where to go?

There is a lot of that – ghost companies trundling along without a goal and without much knowledge about their goals and themselves. Guided by the annoying iron rules of three: others have tried this before, it will never work, we have never done it like this before. Obstructing is always possible! Outcome not. Just don't move and anyone who stands out will fall out: out of the community, the self-controlling group that wants other opinions but doesn't tolerate them. A paradise for consultancies. Here, completely new business levels can be reached. Big fees per day per hour, guaranteed lack of change, thus no outcome. But everyone has a good feeling for themself, they were actively involved. Best: spontaneously active. Or even agile. Hectic! Just don't think about it, in the end something useful would come out of it. Maybe a few jobs were lost, but it never hit the wrong people and never someone from the leadership.

There he sat, had changed a company again and everything started all over again. At zero; no, this time even below zero. In the range of minus, the typical minus area from a ghost company.

There was even less here than in the last company. Which is hard to describe, as if you had a task, like cleaning up a flat. Then, you open the front door, and the first room is empty. The second room is empty, and the third room is also deserted. The rooms after that weren´t built at all, Potemkin villages. Well, the walls of the first rooms are dirty and it smells.

However the task was to tidy up, not to paint or build up the rest. He stood in a flat, or rather a company, and realized: even the nothingness was not there. Everything was lacking! What he had been upset about in other companies before; here he didn't even find any fuss; within himself and certainly not from his colleagues. The processes were not ready yet. The standard saying.

More precisely: there were no processes. Yes, hadn't he guessed that in the interview, his friends had asked him. Wasn't there any talk about a difficult environment? Yes, they had!

Exactly those words had been used: difficult environment. Apparently, everyone knew what it meant, except him. Maybe he just defined a difficult environment differently, not as something annoying, but as something solvable. He spoke clearly and not in riddles. Until now, he was always part of a solution, in all companies. Here he was now the problem. He was new. A solution not sought. He was disturbing. Not only did his thoughts grow blacker, so did his mood. Day after day, hour after hour.

Every scary film contained more cheerfulness. Even in a pitch-black cellar, at three in the morning, things were more cheerful. Cheerful, light-hearted, joyful, happy, exhilarated beautiful contrasts to his current mood. His mood was simply lousy. The cat is out of the bag!

An increase, rather a fall into the bottomless pit, seemed no longer possible for him. But as always; it worked without a hitch. If you think you're finished, you're far from it. Don't worry, it goes deeper, sillier. This one session was the final trigger. In a nutshell, it was about nothing, but continuously and for a long time. With a frightening realization: everyone in this company was afraid. Afraid of the customer! Full of fear. His presentation showed one thing above all. The money, advertising expenses and company gifts were distributed to the wrong people. All the data on this was public. He only used what the others did not want to see: Despite the horrendous sums of money, there was no evidence of success or an increase in turnover.

On the contrary: the higher the investment, the lower the ... no, no increase. There were even losses with these clients. Low losses and customers with not even low losses, the company really paid for it! What madness. The clients were happy to take the money. Gladly even a little more every year. To derive an obligation from that is very presumptuous; it wasn't the customers who said that, it was his line managers tone.

Even when he repeated it in his own words, thinking it was generally understandable: >Our sales force gives away money and rewards the customers who only pick up! No customer who has received any form of gratuity in recent years has bought anything from us!< His new colleagues thought that was a bit exaggerated. Even if it was true. There was no question of exaggeration or even *overkill*.

All blind, deaf and silent in one room. But the worst thing was: he was one of them. Of course, a nightmare does not end so easily! During the break, his colleagues took him aside. Their attempts to bring him into line were clear. >Now slow down, colleague ...<, > ... there is always another side to the story ...<, > ... what you see and what I see is not what others see in us ...<, > ... we don't earn badly, think about what you are putting at risk .... <, >. ... just shut up, keep still your feet ...<, > ...young horses trotting behind the old ones...<, >Eeh?<, >This means, too young and too clever<, >Oh!<, > ... bit of a lout, bit of a bully-boy ... <, >The peoples favorite is often a well-meaning fool, no background and no bottom!<, > ...you are virtually provoking McKinsey and Co to come ...< and more. Fortunately, it was a short break. The colleagues continued to press him massively, but he managed to escape into the seminar room.

And all attempts to urge him to restrain himself failed anyway. He would not want to understand, he would not give up, not so quickly! He was still new, still had a chance. He was still in the honeymoon phase of the early days, though here it was more like Halloween with an uncertain outcome.

He remembered a saying by the American inventor Edison: Many failures in life are due to the fact that people did not know how close they were to the goal when they gave up. He saw himself very close to the goal: Every rain begins with single drops.

The drama didn´t come to an end, not even in the second part of the session. The third act seemed far from being reached. Shakespeare's hamlet still in full glory. Again, it was about customers, again about the fear of losing existing non-customers. >Losing zero turnover means that the result remains zero; or am I wrong?< The question couldn´t be clarified, his boss did not even address it. Not only that, he also no longer paid any attention to him at all. As if he had said nothing. His boss no longer noticed him, his colleagues followed their boss. Nobody seemed to hear or want to hear his >Hello?< either. After all, it had taken him three years to get to this state in the old company, here not even six weeks. But was that his goal? Didn't he want to make a difference? Where were the drops that started the rain now?

What he wanted to move, however, he was no longer sure of either. The lack of goals seemed to be a contagious disease. In any case, his colleagues treated him just like a contagious disease. Well. There are worse things than that.

Then he was the plague. Once the reputation is ruined ... he stood up, in the middle of the sentence of the almighty marketing manager: >There is no point in blathering on here about assumptions that are far removed from reality. At least mine are! < >Mr ...<, the marketing manager said. In any case, he had not remembered his name. It got even better: pour some oil into the indignation, no more feigning inhibition. >If you had been present at my presentation, you would know what I am talking about. Nothing in this company makes a profit. The sales department doesn't. Your marketing doesn't. The products alone are great. And they sell themselves. Even without your phantom show!< Now there was no one at the meeting whom he had not accused of failure, incompetence or worse. He now stood there defenseless, all alone. Seemingly surrounded, however: an older colleague also stood up. >Where our freshman is right, he is right. We don't bother our customers excessively and they order! We don't ask, they order. Often, we even avoid our customers. Still, they order. Our products are good.< A murmur went around the room, everyone could agree on that. A little peace, take a breath. He sat down, his offensive had fizzled out, arbitrariness took over. At the end of the meeting, the boss asked him to come with him straight away, to his office. Self-satisfied faces accompanied his departure.

>What was that?< the general manager began immediately. >You didn't move anything. That was not the deal. You were supposed to, no, you wanted to turn everything upside down. Turn the pyramid upside down. Raise potentials. And now? The goal heads have won again. That was really quite differently agreed upon!"

He looked at him and said nothing. In the meeting not giving an opinion, not helping him, and now this! >We agreed something different, that's true. And it applies to both of us, you and me. I didn't realize you were supporting me. I didn't even notice that you wanted any change at all. I saw the fear in your eyes and I still see it. It won't work like that!<

The general manager looked at him: >That's our problem: nobody dares to do anything. The salespeople are afraid of the customers, the department heads are afraid of the salespeople, the marketing department is afraid of the sales force and I'm no better. We need you; otherwise nothing will move here.< These words reconciled him and resonated for a long time. He was needed after all, he had known it, his boss wanted change. Poo Hoo, it wasn't all for nothing.

The general manager opened the balcony door: >Would you have a cigarette with me?< >No thanks, non-smoker.< >Oh, please, at least join us. Our peace pipe. < There was nothing wrong with that, he couldn't stand in the smoke. They both went out.

Of course, the office was on the top floor, so of course the view was fantastic. The boss lit his cigarette and took a deep drag: once, twice, three times. Then he exhaled deeply and for a long time. Until then he enjoyed the yellow-reddish sun, it bathed the city in a shining gold. To live here, to stand here, was a gift. Full of poison.

He couldn't take it all so much to heart, become more relaxed. Not to take his boss too seriously. Otherwise, his job would kill him. Suddenly he felt a violent jolt to his back, fell forward, couldn't hold on to the railing and screamed. Ten seconds later he crashed onto the concrete of the street, bones splintered, two cars crashed into each other. Between them lay a lifeless male body.

>There's some truth in that: I have more fear of our customers than of a murder. Crazy!< the boss said to himself >When he was right, he was right!<

stay behind
Mikos Meininger 2017

As a boss it was like this: Sickness did not exist! Not only was it not worth it: there was simply no scope for illness in the budget forecast. >The third quarter went badly, I was ill.< Who would want to show off like that? Wikler not, at any rate. Nevertheless: Wikler didn't like Wikler very much. His body surrendered to time. But it wasn't. He didn't like his body, it was a foreigner to him, his soul searching asylum in inner parts of his frame, this had been for over fifty years. There was no reason to change it.

From time to time, came new colleagues, all of them captivating with relaxed skill. He simply admired them. Wikler, on the other hand, adapted to company goals. Wikler was still there.

The colleagues came and went. They were interested in their time, they served excellently as stooges. The hands of their clock were racing; their time was running out before they knew it. So Wilker always did what a man should do: - to stand his ground. If necessary, he would liquidate. All the older colleagues were afraid of Wikler. A conversation with him could always mean an exit. His bent body behind the desk hid the tension that was in him. Until their own dismissal, these new colleagues did not take him seriously or even notice him. It always resulted in their demise.

Sometimes, his irresistible youthful smile still flashed, but then immediately froze on his face. Afterwards, his body radiated a listlessness that showed only one thing: in old age, method triumphs over skill and knowledge. A lot of things just seemed sad. His carefully arranged office took the visitors' breath away. Alone, not to disturb the less than tasteful arrangement.

Since the weekend, a giant hogweed (Heracleum mantegazzianum) from his garden stood by the window, it loved the sun, like himself. It was a huge umbellifer. Wikler liked the extra protection from the sun. The herb grew imposingly.

He liked that kind of thing: clear rules, clear processes. Water and sun equal strong growth. He could live with that. His processes were sacred to him. He observed them strictly and ruthlessly. Processes broke resistance, broke people. That is why Wikler loved processes, especially his own processes.

The price of a share is driven by imagination and hope. Wikler lubricated the clockwork behind it so that the cogs would mesh smoothly. So that dreams remained dreams.

He knew that his department was superbly staffed, right down to the supporting roles. A desire for recognition next to youthful recklessness, overconfidence without expertise, unscrupulousness, however, without danger to himself. If you can do it, you can do it, Wikler thought. Even his best man looked like the image of a Romanian pickpocket. Pretty sure Romanians feared him too. His best buddy sat next to him; he came into the office in every morning like a drunk from the corner pub. Maybe from the >The Rose&Crown< across the street or from >The Queens dead<, sorry, >The Queens Head<, vis-á-vis. Another would also pass for a blackmailer. In any case, they both were devoid of competence.

His department was considered difficult. Like Wikler himself, after all. Few discovered this charm of eternal haggling among themselves. They did not even understand the advantages. So he took responsibility without the burden of real decisions. Someone was always ambitious enough to take on this or that task. This manual skill, his own manual skill, Wikler found it brilliant and vulgar.

A healthy human relationship consisted of communication, self-love and someone who took responsibility. Three things he allowed to be passively shaped. Also, privately in his marriage. After the separation of his first wife, he lived alone for three years. The second marriage also proved dysfunctional. The third wife did not stay for six months. Now he had understood. He applied this communication principle everywhere, it worked. He let it run its course. In the company as well as in the marriage.

His greatest success: He was even able to integrate a young woman into this bunch of the department. Rather, she quickly adapted herself. Three children forced compromises. Tall, slim, dark-haired. What exactly she worked at, Wikler did not know at all. In any case, her tasks were precarious. He was sure of that and conveyed it in every conversation with the HR department. Power grew with the number of their own employees. Her greatest shortcoming was the germs she brought and spread. Her children got everything. In a Kindergarten, a germ was probably bred until even the strongest antibiotics were helpless. No disease control authority cared!

First it killed the entire department in January. When all the places were finally occupied again, the next bacterial lobe came, then scarlet fever. In April, she somehow seemed fresher than usual, then suddenly keeled over the next day. The fainting spell was just a circulatory disorder. But everyone who had touched her got a rash afterwards. By mid-May, all the colleagues were back, the department complete. Visibly weakened, with no further immune defense. Some colleagues were already speculating that this year, in addition to swine fluv in the fattening farms, there would also be child plague in the kindergartens. But no one is allowed to know that. Three children in two different kindergartens offered a rich, rarely large reservoir of pests, bacteria and germs. Only the mother herself seemed exhausted but immune. Often, she just seemed happy. And she did not disturb Wikler in his work. Wikler did not get sick. Score!

Because each completed forecast was only the prelude to the next one. And the emptier the department, the more time Wikler had for the important things in working life: signing off budgets, releasing funds, drawing up plans, discarding them, forging new ones, and spreading cheer every quarter. The work didn't stop, the fewer disruptive factors were present, the better the processes ran.

And a cold does not knock a manager down. May the employees take time off and pay homage to their illnesses; whether imaginary or real. The next forecast was not waiting. Wikler would rather do without a tie and collar and come to work in a thick jumper. The main thing was that things rolled along. Developed further. Stagnation was death. A rolling stone gathers no moss. Wikler, as the boss, was aware of his role model function. Also, in the fight against the child killer bugs. What time off would the employees take if the boss were simply absent? That was dangerous. More dangerous than such an insignificant germ. Missing forecasts, i.e., missing successes, threatened the department and especially its head much more.

So now it's time for the mid-year feedback talks, which internally are called Mid-Year Talks. The young mother was the first. Wikler was sure that this interview would be a pleasure. That wasn't always the case for a supervisor with the pile of interviews.

She came into the office and seemed unsettling with her sensationally fresh manner. Now it was clear to him what he found so fascinating about her: this willingness to take a risk, to be the first to have the mid-year talk with him. Her curiosity and her orderliness. She had a whole pile of clear plastic sheets with her. Wikler was all restless, it looked like processes! He loved procedures, he loved processes. He felt warm all over.

117

She sniffled and coughed around a bit before sitting down, >Nothing big. The little one wasn't allowed in the nursery. My husband is looking after her today. Just a bit of a fever.< The danger of this statement passed Wikler by, he still felt quite strangely warm. He was sweating. She went on the offensive, started with her tasks, her solutions and made suggestions. Showed graphs and texts. Her work: a complete success!

Wikler couldn't quite understand it, he was preoccupied with himself. His arm itched terribly and his neck too. Maybe he couldn't tolerate her perfume. But she didn't smell as a scent cloud of perfume at all. Or had he now contracted it from her too. His opinion of her wavered. He didn't want to see these child killer bugs near him for a moment longer. He struggled to breathe.

>Are you all right?< she asked him abruptly. How? Spreading her germs, or more precisely, those of her children and the death germs of the nursery in his office, which was bursting with health. How could he be well there? Now the sun was shining into his office, the heat was almost unbearable. He went to the window and opened it, catching his hand on his giant hogweed. The killer bacterium-woman was still sitting at his desk and coughing: >As if I suddenly had bronchitis!< she said.

He stayed at the window a little longer. The sun was good for him. Like a curtain, the growing dislike of this walking bacterium drew itself between them. Wikler scratched his hand. It burned, he scratched harder. The whole hand looked like it had been burnt. Red and full of blisters. Wikler doubled over. No, they're not done yet, he was still thinking. An assessment interview consisted not only of comfortable topics, but also of motivating speech, revealing flaws and desires. Talked out in both directions. He could hardly breathe; his thoughts were fleeting. In the background he only heard a soft cough. His spirit disappeared with his consciousness.

>A giant hogweed? This plant is poor poison! Who puts something like that in their office?< the paramedic was speechless: >We're taking him to pathology now.< >It was a gift after all. From the garden! Full of love. From his wife. He was bombastically proud of it< said the secretary: >He never wanted to part from her again! She was his great love at last.< > Then they have now separated.<

>This is pure poison!< the paramedic repeats. >Poison?< suspected a policeman. >Hard to prove.< answered the paramedic. >Never, not a bit!< said the policeman.

>This is pure poison!< the paramedic repeats to himself. They are answered by a dry cough in the back of the room. And another barely audible female voice follows: >Poison, how creepy!<

stay onside
Mikos Meininger 2017

Kill him

This man has to go. The inevitability of this thought seemed increasingly urgent to Hans Holmst. At first the thought came to him once every three months, then three times in one month. Now three times a day: This man has to go!

This man has just entered his office. Went to the copier, put in new paper, copied, and went out again. Now the rest of the day Hans Holmst was dominated by one idea: Away! Away with him! But how?

In the evening, without a word or a greeting, he walked past his wife into the kitchen. He took his bottle of beer, made himself a sandwich with sausage, sat down on the couch and stared at the flat screen all evening. No lovely word for his lovely wife.

Around midnight he went to bed. The whole evening without saying a sound. His wife looked at Hans with concern. He had changed in the last few months. The loving and concerned man, always concerned about her, developed into a taciturn man. A man who hardly noticed his surroundings. He also no longer talked to anyone. He sat next to her and yet was in his own world. Continents away. Another sad evening.

Hans, on the other hand, went to bed in a cheerful mood.

His last beer had provided the solution. This thought had been in the air for so long and Hans, with one of the last sips, had dissolved the last obstacle, the practical implementation. As he stared at the screen, his thoughts circled around only one person, and around his plan. This person had to go. Now he knew how: kill him. Slowly.

With this feelings Hans and his wife fell asleep with the same thought, tomorrow they would tackle it and change their lives. Hans woke up early, saw his wife sleeping, quietly got ready and left. On the dresser he left her a note: I love you!

His wife lay awake in bed half the night. When she noticed that Hans woke up, she pretended to be asleep. She watched him get dressed and leave. It was then that she realized how much she missed him. His loving concern, his jokes, his touches. She still loved him.

In the office, Hans appeared first. The empty desks in the large room radiated an unexpected calm. A calm that Hans needed now, with which he went purposefully about his work. Hans fetched the form

"Personnel Request/Description ID" from the shared L-drive and filled it out conscientiously. He only gave very good marks. At the end, he put his decisive sentence under remarks: Due to the constant under-demand and excellent task performance, an immediate transfer to a suitable position is of the greatest benefit to our company. Otherwise, I consider an exodus of this high potential possible at any time.

Calmly and quietly, Hans read through the personnel sheet again. He smiled. The conclusion from this assessment seemed only logical. ID applied to special cases alone, urgent, and acute. This case was pressing Hans, it was more than acute. This man had to go.

Satisfied with himself and the world, he lay back in his office chair and printed out the "Personnel Request/Description ID ". Skimmed it one more time and put it in the basket, in a red folder.

Red folder meant urgent, reserved only for the big fishes! Hans thought deportation was better than, for example, murder. And it really wouldn't have taken much more. Hans knew that this process would now fall like an like an avalanche down the mountain. Slowly, a small stone rolled down until no one stood in the way of this elemental force. His little stone that made the mountain slide was called Personnel Request/Description ID! This collective incompetence, know-it-all attitude and nagging would soon come to an end.

The manager's son neatly shoved off. The champagne corks were popping in Hans imagination. I wonder which department got him now? Anyway, it was none of Hans' business anymore. The late riser didn't show up before eleven o'clock anyway.

Maybe he should write an e-mail to his new colleagues, give them a heads-up.

>Mrs Holmst<, it is a pleasure to meet you personally for once. Please take a seat!<

The manager led Ms Holmst to a seating area. It still seemed like a miracle to Mrs Holmst. This morning she called the manager's secretary and got an appointment right away. Yes, it was only possible today, there was no more free appointments for the next three weeks. The managing director would be at the company's headquarters in Toronto for another week after that. So today!

>What brings you here?< asked the managing director. And Ms Holmst told, hesitantly at first. But soon she gained she had confidence and it bubbled out of her. Her husband, always so attached to his job, the perfect loving husband had changed so much in the last few months. She didn't recognize him. I wonder if it had something to do with his work. Had something changed in his job? The manager promised her he would take care of it today. Mrs Holmst left and her heartbeat loudly in her chest. She was glad that she had summoned up all her courage. Now every-thing would be like it used to be.

The manager pinpointed the moment of Mr Holmst's change as the day he shoved his son into his department.

The whining brat had enormous potential. Especially when it came to getting on someone's nerves. He had had no qualms about the calm and even-tempered Holmst. His son, however, avoided any social skills. He had to free Holmst. And he wanted to reward him too. He fetched a "personnel requisition/ description ID" from the collection drive and rewarded Hans Holmst with a better job in another department. This position in the newly created department had been vacant for three months and the company needed a professional. Someone like Hans Holmst. Then the department only lacked an overall head. This matter with Mr Holmst cost him two hours.

When he returned to his office, his busy schedule was pressing. First, he signed the red folders. By now they were piling up on his desk. Next to them, he tried to process his emails. As a result, he gave neither the mails nor the red folders his full attention. And also signed Hans Holmst's input.

While the managing director was in Toronto, the whole company relaxed. Hans Holmst had been able to move the son and for a fortnight he had also been back at home as before.

A nice feeling of happiness spread through Mrs Holmst. This was the right man, she had chosen the man of her dreams. Then the personnel manager asked Hans to come in. He spilled the beans about the great opportunity of promotion in the company, personally arranged by the managing director. More responsibility, better salary, better company car. Did he want to take this job? Hans finally felt recognized. And said yes. In the evening the Holmsts celebrated. They went to the first restaurant on the square, and it was also a wonderfully relaxed and exuberant evening. Nothing reminded him of the late riser anymore, whichever department was suffering from him now.

The next day, the personnel manager took Hans to his new department. His new boss would always be a little late. Everyone laughed.

Hans Holmst was amazed at where his input had led this rascal. He felt sick. A steep climb, even for the son of a managing director. His first and only thought: I have to leave! Or kill myself.

stay inside
Alexander Schaal 2020

Finally, the last dance

At thirty something, you are discarded. Dancers can work a few months longer, but for women it's finally finished. Wendy looked at herself in the mirror, three months to go. But her face said it abundantly clear: You are dead. Today! Wendy calmly faced this fact. Saying goodbye is the last part of a career. It's only a stage that dies, she reassured herself. Not yourself. But that was all she had lived for over twenty years: their stage. The applause that would not end. The stage curtains that were counted. Fans who waited for her for hours, she wanted to be adored. Of course, she had complained about it all these years, but it was never real. She loved being the centre of attention, and the centre of attention she was! This enigmatic stage personality dies and all that is left is Wendy, an unknown entity to herself.

Every day she could transform a new metamorphosis, be exhausting and still be adored. A star is allowed to do that. A dazzling body bathed in applause, the saint, sometimes drama, sometimes not. No one knew for sure. Often not even she. Now she had to give up her own profession, start all over again. She felt it all: fear for irrelevance, fear of the future, fear of isolation, fear of being abandoned and fear to be excluded from this world and left it, with a new start in a world she didn't understand, had never touched before.

Wendy had subordinated her whole life to dance, time, effort, pain. Heavy investment with no monetary return.

Overnight it would be finished. Poof, the next stars were ready. Men didn't even look down her neckline anymore. It starts at four, then from seventeen the folk pay to enter. The first bleeding doesn't come until twenty-five. First no woman, and later no woman again. She could go on for another year or two, but her body could barely manage it now: three and a half hours of ballet.

Only the abstainers who had happily made it through life without injuries could manage that. Wendy's list of fractures and torn tendons was long. She didn't even count minor injuries. She could no longer wear normal shoes; her feet were so bent today.

Reality was always everything outside the dancefloor for Wendy, she dreaded it. Never spent too much time on that being real, what was real, reality? The bouquets of flowers in the dressing room, the war between the dancers as soon as a man wasn't gay, the offers from the old rich men who wanted to lock her away like a tiger in the zoo? Once she found the love of her life. That was real. And he was gone before it really began! It's the reality that's off-putting. The surgeons were just taking apart her right hip, drilling it open to patch the acetabular lip, only the hammering afterwards was worse. But he was already fleeing when the first blood flowed over her snow-white skin. >I'm so weak!< he just said and disappeared. Right, what a wimp! She, on the other hand, fought her way back from the operating table to the stage. Got better than ever. And then came the opiates. First for the pain, then for her life, in the end to survive.

Wendy and her make-up table: she draws her eyeliner perfectly with the matter-of-factness and carefulness that others put on their panties. She smiles wryly at herself, letting the water in her beautiful light blue eyes drain inwards. In the dressing room she sits alone, that is status. Hard won, danced for. She used to think she would rather die than stop dancing. Today she knew it is.

Her farewell dance yesterday lasted ninety minutes, ninety minutes of pure happiness. Rousing applause. Praise and rapture today in the feuilleton. Simply the energy of her life danced in perfect lust and abandon, rewarded and cheered with euphoria. She wrestles with herself, for air, wrestles with her future. Afterwards, her director came, hugged and kissed her; said into the jubilation that he had taken her off the cast list. After one of her greatest successes! She asked him why? >She would soon not live up to his standards. He would prevent her from embarrassing herself in front of the audience. That would be even more painful than saying goodbye today.< he said. No conversation before, no plan together, no advice for the future. Wendy looked at the syringe and the packet of heroin beside it on her make-up table. She could end it right now. Forever. That thought alone is a deep delight.

After opiates came heroin. But with heroin came hepatitis. Bad handle and contact included. Her coach freed her, sent her to rehab and again Wendy fought her way back onto the stage. Even if her body's coordination sometimes failed, she was still better than all the other girls.

The whole cold system, only the strongest survived here. Wendy was strong! The coach who used to grab her between her legs when she was a girl and humiliate her, whose shoes she had to lick with her tongue when she failed a jump. All the other abuse, all long forgotten. Only success counted. After the sexual abuse of various coaches, she switched to a female coach. Here she felt safe. Until this trainer beat her fingers with a long rod if Wendy failed to do something. Wendy rarely failed, but then the trainer could be in a bad mood and hit her anyway. Sometimes like this, sometimes like that. She consoled herself with the not too far future of stardom. But even as a star, the coach kept hitting Wendy, again and again. Wendy was not granted a happy ending. The heroin laughed at her. Just one shot, quickly cooked, injected, died - all would end peacefully.

Everything else would just be jobs: ballet mistress or teacher. Exercises just to fight the boredom of daily being, banal pilates, gyrotonics, physiotherapy, yoga, osteopathy or similar meaningless professions, hollow things without charm. Finding the right thing can take time. Heroin, on the other hand, works immediately. She smiled. From the dazzling bubble of dance, into the soapy bubble of a drug baroness. Yes, she liked that. A female Narco. No really, she bristled, it didn't matter to her fate whether she lived another year or not. Mentally she was stronger than all those junkies. Her coach had said she should take her time, quietly think for a year before making a decision. This year she would lead it. Wendy would supply the entire ballet, the stagehands, the directors. A fine little market with a big turnover.

This heroin and that syringe could wait another year. It was she who decided when to stop, not some limp-wristed director. The sovereignty was hers, self-determined. Besides, she knew he also took opiates. For pain. He didn't know yet how much heroin would help him. The first fix was it. Nothing else came close to that, after that all addicts just searched. Stunned themselves and forced the powder hot into their veins. Of course, the heroin would make him addicted. He deserved it. And then step by step it went up for Wendy, like dancing. Not so for the others. But Wendy knew her goal.

She was relaxed when she drew up her plan. She took into account legal, administrative and financial risks. The future would pay her handsomely. As a dancer, as an athlete, she knew exactly when it would hurt where. Which shot had injected at best points of the body to fight the pain. How and where addicts hid their cutlery, arms were covered, the best places for the next injection were. She could provide sound support for sports medicine strength training, well dosed to prevent premature caries. She would make the most money from the long-term criminals, no – long-term dancers. She would focus on choreography and sell her drugs. Finally get revenge on all the abuse that had happened to her. A great plan. That's why she wasn't a junkie: clear thoughts, a better plan and full control over her life. Wendy felt strong, like she hadn't in a long time in her life.

And then Wendy took the sack of heroin, boiled it up and injected herself. The entire bag.

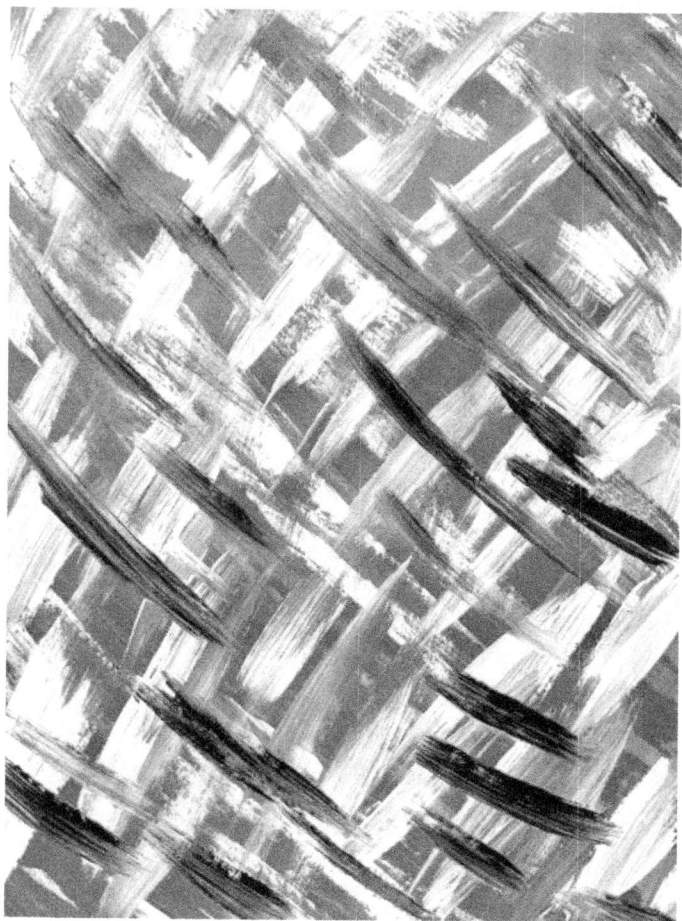

stay around
Alexander Schaal 2020

also available

our man in outer space

launched in 2022, april.

Crystal Teeth

This light irritated him from the very beginning. Above the eyes, sitting in the middle, was a thread of skin only a few millimetres thick spouted from the forehead, a very firm, flexible thread that hung forward in an arc and ended in a large luminous sphere. It glowed, sometimes strongly, sometimes weaker, in all the colours of the multi-universe. Somehow it expressed the state of the creature's mind or feelings. Or, something else entirely. Two beings sat opposite him. Both were glowing in front of him. If he bent forward, the intensity increased, if he leaned back in his chair, the light dimmed. Interesting. The colours also changed, from rather milky to rather solid. Contact with inhabitants of exoplanets was always difficult, first contacts often went miserably, dismally. Every being after its own kind, this tolerance hardly applied on Earth, and practically zero in space. Anything was possible, at any time. He was used to grief. But, it went quite well with these guys.

Today was the third time they would meet each other. It went ahead. The two guests came from the star system Phobetor. What radiated there was enough energy for our Milky Way for more than millions of years. The people living there tolerated radioactivity excellently. On their home planet, at least twenty Hiroshima-type atomic bombs exploded every second, on every spot of the planet! But they also tolerated our atmosphere quite well, even oxygen. In general, their shape was very close to that of humans. They had a body, extremities, and moved in a way that almost resembled walking. Only the head always reminded him of a deep-sea fish. As soon as they opened their mouths, he felt a little sick to his stomach.

It only shimmered in their mouths, much like the colour of the surroundings. They had no teeth. Humans had only discovered them by accident, during a routine examination on Proxima centauri, where they found an extremity. Something like an arm or so. It was lying there alone, but it was alive. After the examination, people knew of a new species in space: its DNA was 1,000 times more densely packed than human DNA and its repair enzymes 100,000 times faster. At this point, interesting market potential was identified. Maybe even the fulfilment of the dream of eternal life at last. It smelled like money. So, in came the research, the corporations, and the usual adventurers. In reverse order, of course! They were all looking for this species. They found it in the most inhospitable regions of space.

It was difficult to make contact, and the high radiation levels meant that hardly any messages reached the Phobetor system. But one of their transporters intercepted the radio waves on its journey and reported back. Of course, no one on Earth understood what these signals meant, but it was a start. They had a language and something like wave-based communication. And now, here they were, sitting together. He was the expert in extraterrestrial contact and had already established and developed many business relationships. Soon he would be retiring. This one negotiation, then it would be over. In his ear the control centre made an announcement; - they were sitting directly behind him in the next room, behind a glass wall. The glass was made of multiple diamonds and gold-lead inlays. There was no safer material on the market. If things went wrong, he was the pawn. Only with money did things rarely go wrong. All cultures in space wanted to expand their power and wealth, greed trumps everything these days, after all. It made trading a piece of cake. Besides, they had brought Borophen with them. Maybe the DNA did encode things we didn't know about. Well, this belief in a higher power, something god-like, was possessed by all living beings in the universe. Maybe greed too. That would be an exciting research project for his retirement.

Not only did they possess miracle-wound-healing of their bodies, they also possessed Borophene, one of the most interesting materials the universe had to offer. The single layer of boron atoms, together with silver atoms, formed a flat, two-dimensional hexagonal structure. But most of the boron atoms only bonded with four or five atoms., thus, space was left in between the gaps. This gap pattern is what made Borophene so special. More stable than Graphene but much more flexible! It had almost no weight of its own

but was extremely reactive and also superconductive with water, heat and electricity. It stored more than fifteen percent of its own weight in hydrogen. This storage capacity was needed everywhere in space.

The left creature opposite him began to spread tonal waves. It took two seconds and it was translated to him: >We shit in peace, as subjects of the Delxis. We hunt trade.< Well, this translation was not yet perfect, but it was enough for simple communication. If he modify shit with sit and hunt with seek or look for it makes sense.

He said: >We are also a peaceful group that likes to trade.< Both of them slid back, their eyes shining a hazy red and bodies tense, almost poised for attack. He was wondering what the translator had made of his words. Calmly he adds once again: >Peace and trade.< >Then trade in us off!< replied one, or better the other creature, to his right. He did not see any genders. >What do you want to trade in?< he asked. >People.< said the left creature. >Humans!< said the other.

He was amazed, no one had expected that. Silence. >We want food. Flesh.< >Human flesh?< >Maybe the translation is wrong. We want food.< He breathed a sigh of relief, for a rare, strange fear had taken hold of him. Now all was well again. >We grow meat, we make it in the pressure robot, and we even have meatless meat.< he said and in the control room they congratulated him on how he had got his act together. >We know. This is Borophen, whole ship is full. Give us meat. Quickly.< That was a direct negotiating style for once. But he liked it better than this diplomatic back and forth. >How much meat do you want for it?< >Three humans!< said the left creature. >No is a mistake, three human-sized meats.< >We can offer you cattle, they are even bigger than humans. Or elephants. Very tender, juicy meat.< >Well, you get ship load of Borophen, we get meat from planets here.<

Now he was confused, this translation programme had major flaws after all.

Something pulled his left negotiator out of his mouth, and open he looked even more comical, more impressive. As if the lower jaw was folded out, like a snake before it swallows a donkey. In the mouth he saw a fleshy tongue of similar substance to the outer skin and no teeth. How were they going to eat the meat? Perhaps they had claws on their hands. He looked carefully at the table. No, he didn't see any claws either. All in all, pretty peaceful carnivores when he compared them to humans. More like the pigs of the universe, omnivores. He was enjoying the negotiation more and more. If it was really that easy and successful, he would have a nice extra pension for his old age. He was a lucky man.

These thoughts were also his last. The alien head with its open jaw shot forward, wrapped itself completely around his head and closed. His body did not even twitch. Blood flowed from the left creature's mouth. His partner stood up and paced the room. Nervous, hungry, full of drive. He licked his lips. Searched further. The control room behind the glass wall was silent. >That went pretty wrong.< someone said. Suddenly astonished: >Oh, they do have teeth.< >Apparently made of glass.< >Or crystal?< >In any case transparent!< There was a dull crash, the glass shattered. Now they saw one of the left creature's teeth shining dully, it had smashed through the pane of the wall. It continued to snap it jaws towards the helpless humans. >They meant human flesh after all!< Behind the team suddenly stood the second one, his open mouth shining, he smiled as he said: >Human! Delicious.<

The program didn't translate that badly.

Real is:

The material graphene, which has excited researchers, is a material made of a single layer of carbon atoms. The hype has died down, but the interest in a two-dimensional material remained. The next material candidate became borophene[1]. A single layer of boron atoms. The fact that this material even existed was predicted by computer simulations in the years around 1990. In 2015, physicists were able to synthesise it for the first time. In vapour deposition, hot gas of boron atoms is condensed onto a cool surface of pure silver. This forces the boron atoms into a pattern similar to silver, a flat hexagonal structure. Out of six possible bonds, boron uses only four or five. This gap pattern gives borophene crystals their special properties. Borophene is more stable than graphene, and at the same time more flexible, conducts electricity and heat, is superconducting, light and reactive! The material is interesting, for example, for batteries and accumulators. Borophene can store more than fifteen percent of its weight in hydrogen, which is significantly more than other materials. As a catalyst, it is also able to decompose molecular hydrogen.

Great white shark or piranha teeth are comparably hard and sharp[2]. In the deep sea, the dragonfish is an efficient predator, as it has equally sharp and hard but also transparent sabre teeth[3]. In the deep sea, food is scarce and many creatures can produce light[4], e.g. to hunt or to orientate themselves. The dragonfish goes the other way, becoming invisible. As an apex predator, it feeds on smaller fish that swim into its relatively large jaws. It can open its jaws wide enough to take in prey up to 50 percent of its own size. Its jaw muscle is weak, however, so it needs sharp, large fangs to bore into the prey. They are narrow, pointed and effective. The teeth are too large for the jaw and protrude from the mouth. Their surface makes them appear transparent or highly translucent. Its teeth consist of a layer of dentin covered by collagen fibrils, it reduces the scattering of light. The surface of the teeth is smooth and striped. Only the striated sections of the dentin layer are rough and consist of longitudinal stripes and ridges. Tubules, which otherwise colour the dentin, are missing. Compared to human teeth, the teeth are more mineralised and harder. The dragonfish disappears into the background as it swims through the water, hunting its prey using its own invisibility.

References

1 Yusuf Valentino Kaneti et al. Borophene: Two-dimensional Boron Monolayer: Synthesis, Properties, and Potential Applications. In *Chem. Rev.* 2022, 122, 1, 1000–1051 Publication Date:November 3, 2021 https://doi.org/10.1021/acs.chemrev.1c00233 Copyright © 2021 American Chemical Society and https://pubs.acs.org/doi/10.1021/acs.chemrev.1c00233

2 Neighbors M.A. Nafpaktitis B.G. Lipid compositions, water contents, swimbladder morphologies and buoyancies of nineteen species of midwater fishes (18 myctophids and 1 neoscopelid) Mar. Biol. 1982; 66: 207-215

3 Audrey Velasco-Hogan, Dimitri D. Deheyn, Marcus Koch, Birgit Nothdurft, Eduard Arzt, Marc A. Meyers. On the Nature of the Transparent Teeth of the Deep-Sea Dragonfish, Aristostomias scintillans. Matter, Published: June 05, 2019 DOI: https://doi.org/10.1016/j.matter.2019.05.010

4 Haddock S.H.D. Moline M.A. Case J.F 6. Bioluminescence in the sea. Ann. Rev. Mar. Sci. 2010; 2: 443-493 http://www.annualreviews.org/doi/10.1146/annurev-marine-120308-081028

More books by the author via amazon kindle:, only in german

ISBN: 9783981928198   1x täglich. Ein ganzer Monat mit 31
                       Kalenderblättern

Reihe *Mord ist auch nur ein Wort*

ISBN: 9781090529145   Band 1, keine kleinen Morde

ISBN: 9781076929433   Band 2, feiste Finsterlinge for future

ISBN: 9781077870710   Band 3, kein Seerosenteich ist unschuldig

ISBN: 9798651765324   Band 4, Notiz Buch

ISBN: 9798652010287   Band 5, Der gestorbene Schnurrbart

Science-Fiction Storys

ISBN: 9781075988172   All unser Wissen ist Alltag im All,